Candy Fairies

#3

3-Books-in-1!

READ ALL THE CANDY FAIRIES BOOKS!

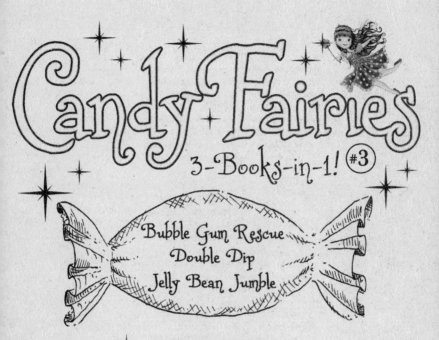

Candy Fairies

3-Books-in-1! #3

Bubble Gum Rescue
Double Dip
Jelly Bean Jumble

HELEN PERELMAN

ILLUSTRATED BY
ERICA-JANE WATERS

ALADDIN
NEW YORK LONDON TORONTO SYDNEY NEW DELHI

ALADDIN

An imprint of Simon & Schuster Children's Publishing Division
1230 Avenue of the Americas, New York, New York 10020
This Aladdin paperback edition December 2017
Bubble Gum Rescue text copyright © 2012 by Helen Perelman
Bubble Gum Rescue interior illustrations copyright © 2012 by Erica-Jane Waters
Double Dip text copyright © 2012 by Helen Perelman
Double Dip interior illustrations copyright © 2012 by Erica-Jane Waters
Jelly Bean Jumble text copyright © 2013 by Helen Perelman
Jelly Bean Jumble interior illustrations copyright © 2013 by Erica-Jane Waters
Cover illustrations copyright © 2013 by Erica-Jane Waters
All rights reserved, including the right of reproduction in whole or in part in any form.
ALADDIN and related logo are registered trademarks of Simon & Schuster, Inc.
For information about special discounts for bulk purchases, please contact
Simon & Schuster Special Sales at 1-866-506-1949 or business@simonandschuster.com.
The Simon & Schuster Speakers Bureau can bring authors to your live event.
For more information or to book an event contact the Simon & Schuster Speakers Bureau
at 1-866-248-3049 or visit our website at www.simonspeakers.com.
Series designed by Karin Paprocki and Karina Granda
The text of this book was set in Berthold Baskerville Book.
Manufactured in the United States of America 1117 OFF
2 4 6 8 10 9 7 5 3 1
Library of Congress Control Number 2017932769
ISBN 978-1-5344-1073-2 (pbk)
ISBN 978-1-4424-2218-6 (*Bubble Gum Rescue* eBook)
ISBN 978-1-4424-2220-9 (*Double Dip* eBook)
ISBN 978-1-4424-5298-5 (*Jelly Bean Jumble* eBook)
These titles were previously published individually by Aladdin.

Contents

Bubble Gum Rescue

For Elle Dean Brown,

a choc-o-rific reader at P. S. 6 in NYC

CHAPTER

1

A Sticky Mess

Early in the morning, Melli the Caramel Fairy flew to the top of Caramel Hills. She was checking on the caramel chocolate rolls she had made with her Chocolate Fairy friend Cocoa. Melli smiled at their newest creation drying in the cool shade of a caramel tree. Yesterday the two fairies had worked hard rolling small logs of caramel and then dipping them in chocolate. The final touch was a drizzle of butterscotch on top. Melli couldn't wait to taste one!

A caramel turtle jutted his head out of his shell and smelled the fresh candy. Melli laughed. "You were hiding over by that log," she said to the turtle. She kneeled down next to him. "Did you think you'd snatch a candy without my noticing?"

The turtle quickly slipped his head back into his shell. Still as a rock, he waited to see what the Caramel Fairy would do.

Melli placed one of the candies in front of him. "Of course you may have one," she said sweetly. "There's enough to share."

The turtle stuck his head out again and gobbled it up.

"Do you like the candy?" Melli asked.

The turtle nodded, and Melli smiled. "Cocoa and I are going to bring these to Sun Dip this evening," she said.

Sun Dip was the time at the end of the day when the sun set behind the Frosted Mountains and the Candy Fairies relaxed. Melli loved visiting with her friends and catching up on everyone's activities. And today she and Cocoa would bring their new candy. She hoped her friends would enjoy the sweet treat.

Just as Melli was putting the candies in her basket, she heard a squeal. It sounded like an animal in trouble. She put the basket down and walked toward the sound.

"Hot caramel!" Melli cried as she peered around one of the caramel trees.

Lying on the ground was a small caramella bird. He was trying to flap his wings to fly, but they were barely moving. Melli leaned in closer and noticed that the bird's feathers were wet and stuck together.

Melli reached out to the bird. "You poor thing," she whispered. She tried to calm the little one by talking to him. Caramella birds lived in the valley of Caramel Hills and had bright yellow wing feathers. They lived off the seeds of the caramel trees and filled the hills with their soft chirps.

"Where have you been playing?" Melli asked sweetly. She carefully picked up the bird and gently stroked his head. Immediately she realized that his feathers were covered in thick butterscotch. "How did you get coated in this syrup?" she asked. "No wonder you can't move or fly."

The bird chirped loudly. It was shaking in her hands.

"Butterscotch is not the best thing for feathers," Melli said, smiling at the tiny caramella. "Don't worry, sweetie," she added softly. "Let's give you a good bath and get this mess off your wings. I know all about sticky caramel." She patted the bird's head gently. "I will get you cleaned up in no time. Let's go to the water well and rinse you off."

Melli held on to the bird and flew to the edge of Caramel Hills. The tiny creature seemed to relax in Melli's hands, but his heart was still pounding. At the well Melli began to wash the butterscotch off the bird's wings. She knew she'd have to spend some time scrubbing. She had gotten caramel on her clothes before, and it often took a while to get all the goo off.

After a few rinses Melli began to see his brightly colored feathers.

"There, that does it," she said, feeling satisfied. She stood back and looked at the little bird. "You do have gorgeous yellow wings!"

The bird shook the water off his wings. He was happy to be able to move them freely. He bowed his head to Melli, thanking her for helping him.

"You should be able to fly now," Melli said. "Be careful, and stay away from the sticky stuff!"

"Hi, Melli!" Cocoa appeared next to her. "What are you doing here?"

"Cocoa," Melli gasped. "You scared me! I didn't see you there." She pointed to the caramella bird.

"Look who I found. He was covered in butterscotch, and his wings were stuck together. I just gave him a bath with the fresh well water."

Cocoa's wings fluttered. "Oh, bittersweet chocolate," she said sadly. "This is worse than I thought."

"What are you talking about?" Melli asked. "He's all clean now. He'll be able to fly."

"It's not only this bird I am worried about," Cocoa said. "I heard from a sugar fly that there was a butterscotch syrup spill on the eastern side of Butterscotch Volcano. That must be where this one got syrup on his wings. *All* the caramella birds are in danger!"

"Oh no," Melli said. "So many caramella birds live over there. What else did the sugar fly tell you?"

11

"That was all," Cocoa replied.

Sugar flies passed information around Sugar Valley. If a fairy wanted to get the word out about something important, the sugar flies were the ones to spread the news.

"Let's go now," Melli said urgently. "If Butter-scotch Volcano erupts, there'll be a large spill in the hills." She looked down at the bird. "Is that what happened to you? Will you take us to where you got butterscotch on your wings?"

The bird took flight, and Melli and Cocoa trailed after him. His yellow feathers gleamed in the sunlight. Melli beat her wings faster. She was very concerned about what kind of sticky mess they were going to find.

CHAPTER 2

Butterscotch Volcano

Melli grabbed Cocoa's hand. She couldn't believe the sight below her. Butterscotch Volcano was in the middle of Caramel Hills, and a place where Caramel Fairies often gathered. Once a year at the Butterscotch Festival, a few brave and experienced Caramel Fairies would dip into the volcano for a supply of hot butterscotch.

The extra-sweet syrup was then stored in large barrels in Candy Castle and used throughout the year for special candy projects.

Melli's eyes widened as she saw the thick syrup pooled in the large area east of the volcano. The land was flat, and the caramella birds built their nests there. Now it was a lake of syrupy butterscotch. Melli shook her head in disbelief. Never before had she seen butterscotch ooze out of the volcano. While there was hot butterscotch syrup deep within the volcano, there had not been an eruption in a long, long time.

As Melli flew over the volcano with Cocoa she squeezed her friend's hand tighter. "No wonder that little bird got his feathers sticky," Melli said. She pointed down below—butterscotch was *everywhere*!

"The sugar flies were definitely right about this," Cocoa said. "This is a supersticky mess."

"Did you send the sugar fly to Raina, Berry, and Dash?" Melli asked. If things were this bad, she wanted all her friends to know. Together, the five of them could work to help the caramella birds of Caramel Hills.

Cocoa nodded. "Yes, I sent them each a message," she replied. "I hope they can get here fast."

Melli carefully observed the area. "Look, Cocoa, the butterscotch isn't coming from the *top* of the volcano," she said. She pointed to the top, which was clean and dry. "Where do you think it's coming from?"

Cocoa squinted and then flapped her golden wings. "Let's get a better look," she said bravely.

The two friends flew down closer to the volcano. The sight broke Melli's heart.

"The poor birds," Melli said softly. "This is their home, and now it's a sticky, syrupy mess. "

"They can't even move," Cocoa added. She saw many birds trying to flap their butterscotch-coated wings.

As Melli looked around she suddenly spotted her sister, Cara, perched on a caramel tree. "There's Cara," she said. "Maybe she knows what's going on."

Cara was rubbing a small bird's feathers with a sponge. She was dipping the sponge in a pail of water when Melli and Cocoa landed next to her.

"Oh, Melli!" Cara exclaimed. "I'm so happy you came! We need all the help we can get. This spill is spreading fast."

 17

"How did this happen?" Melli asked. She knelt down next to her sister.

"The volcano cracked, and there's a leak on its side," Cara explained. "I heard the older Caramel Fairies talking."

"Bittersweet," Cocoa muttered.

"All this butterscotch is oozing out of the volcano?" Melli gasped. She shook her head. "This is gooier than I thought!" She held out a little caramel for the bird Cara was cleaning. "Sweet thing," she cooed.

Cara rinsed the bird's feathers again. "This one is going to be okay," she said. "But there are so many others. I'm not sure we'll be able to wash them all."

"That's why *we're* here to help!" Berry said, landing next to Cara.

"We got the sugar fly message," Dash told Melli.

"And we came as fast as we could," Raina added.

Melli was touched that all her friends had gotten to Caramel Hills so quickly. She smiled at the Fruit Fairy, Mint Fairy, and Gummy Fairy standing before her.

The fairies immediately started to care for the butterscotch-coated birds. As they worked Melli kept looking around. The flow of syrup was steady, and the spill was growing larger.

"Raina, why do you think this happened?" Melli asked.

Raina usually had the answers to questions.

She loved to read and was known to have memorized many sections of the Fairy Code Book. The thick volume of the history of Sugar Valley had helped the friends solve mysteries around Candy Kingdom in the past.

"Butterscotch Volcano is dormant," Raina said. "That means it doesn't erupt for long periods of time." She paused and glanced at her friends. "This doesn't mean that it *couldn't* erupt."

"And we know there is butterscotch in there because the fairies filled barrels at the Butterscotch Festival," Dash added.

"Dash is right," Melli agreed. "But it took a week to fill all the barrels at the castle." She glanced over at the volcano. "No, this is very different. I want to go take a closer look. Anyone want to come?"

"I will," Cocoa called. "I've never seen so much butterscotch syrup!"

"We're *all* going with you," Berry said.

Raina and Dash lined up next to the Fruit Fairy. They had finished cleaning a bird and were worried about the amount of syrup too.

All five fairies flew up in the air. Melli took a fast dive near the volcano. Her friends followed.

"Look!" Melli shouted. "There's the crack on the side of the volcano! The older Caramel Fairies were right. It's enormous!"

"No wonder there is an overrun of syrup," Cocoa said.

"A leaky volcano?" Dash asked, wrinkling her nose.

They all looked to Raina. She shrugged. "It can happen," she said. She peered down at the volcano. "Maybe there was an eruption that made the volcano crack?" She tapped her finger to her chin. "That seems the most likely answer."

"Hot caramel," Melli muttered.

"You mean hot butterscotch," Dash said, correcting her.

"This isn't good news at all," Cocoa said.

"No, it's not," Melli replied. She looked at her friends. "The question is, how do we stop this butterscotch burst?"

3

Big Burst

The fairies huddled together on a branch of a caramel tree. From where they were sitting, they could see the butterscotch spreading.

"We have to do something—and fast," Melli said.

"Those poor birds," Raina whispered as she looked below. "The butterscotch in their wings

will keep them from flying. They'll never be able to get food."

Melli felt helpless. Usually she adored Butterscotch Volcano and the rich syrup that was inside. Making candies with the fresh, hot butterscotch was always a highlight of the Butterscotch Festival. Melli loved watching the brave Caramel Fairies dip into the center of the volcano to scoop out the sweet, golden treat. She had never imagined how dangerous the volcano could be!

"The butterscotch is out of control," she said sadly.

Dash flew off the branch and quickly circled the area. When she came back to the branch, she had a sour look on her face. "If we don't stop the leak, the butterscotch will reach Chocolate

Woods. Think of all the animals there—and the chocolate crops!"

"Double-dip bittersweet," Cocoa said, hanging her head.

"We need to stop this," Berry said, sitting down next to Melli.

"Maybe we should be asking *whom* to stop?" Melli asked.

"Mogu?" Cocoa asked. She wrinkled her nose. "Do you think that salty old troll could have done this?"

Melli shivered. The thought of Mogu in Caramel Hills upset her. The greedy troll often tried to steal Candy Fairy candy, but he usually stayed under his bridge in Black Licorice Swamp. She looked to her friends.

"I'm not sure if this is his style," Berry said,

thinking aloud. "The butterscotch from the volcano is yummy, but it's not in candy form. You'd have to do a lot of work to make candy, or have the patience to wait for the butterscotch to cool."

"Doing work and having patience don't seem like Mogu's style," Raina said, agreeing with Berry.

Cocoa fluttered her wings and looked around. "But if Mogu is greedy enough, he might."

"No, Mogu wouldn't be patient enough," Melli said with certainty. "Having patience is one of the hardest parts of being a Caramel Fairy."

"Which is why I like to work with mint," Dash said, grinning. She reached into her pocket and took out a peppermint. "Ahh," she said. "Quick and tasty!"

Melli smiled at her minty friend. No one liked speed better than her friend Dash. She was one of the smallest Candy Fairies, and also one of the fastest. *And* the least patient fairy she knew!

"The more I think about it, I think it's possible the crack just happened naturally," Raina suggested. She slipped the Fairy Code Book out of her bag. "Yes, I have the book," she said to her friends before they could comment. Usually one of her friends couldn't help making fun of her for always having the fact book on hand. In the past the thick volume of the history of Sugar Valley had helped the friends solve mysteries that happened in Candy Kingdom.

"Let's hope there's something in the book that can help us figure out this sticky mess," Melli said.

As the fairies hovered over the book Melli heard her sister call to her.

"Let me go check on Cara," she said to her friends. "I'll be right back."

Down at the bottom of the tree, birds surrounded Cara.

"Melli," Cara gasped when she saw her big sister. "There are so many sticky caramellas! Two Caramel Fairies just left more here for us to clean." Cara's brown eyes were full of tears. "How will we ever save them all?"

Melli hugged her sister. Seeing her so upset made Melli stronger. "We will help one bird at a time," she said. "If we work together, we can figure this out." She pointed up at the tree behind them. "Raina is looking up some facts in the Fairy Code Book. She's sure to find some useful information."

"I hope so," Cara said. "In the meantime, this area will be the rescue center. I'm going to get some more supplies. Can you stay here? I think more caramellas will be coming."

"Sure as sugar, I'll stay," Melli said. She watched her sister fly off, and then she picked up a sticky bird. She carefully wiped its wings and tried to get the syrup off.

Suddenly the sounds of gurgling and rumbling filled the air. It sounded as if a giant was awaking from his slumber. Melli froze. She looked toward the volcano. The crack she had spotted earlier was now split open wider. More butterscotch rolled up to Melli's feet. The spill was getting deeper and deeper . . . and more dangerous for everyone in Caramel Hills.

Cara came up behind her. "Oh no," she

 31

moaned. "More butterscotch! What are we going to do?"

"I'm going to see if the other fairies have come up with a plan," Melli said. "Will you be all right?"

"Yes," Cara said bravely. "I'll work on cleaning the birds. You work on stopping this spill!"

Melli smiled at her little sister. "I'm so proud of you," she said. "I'll try to be back soon."

Soon, she thought, *before this mess gets bigger.*

CHAPTER 4

Chocolate Aid

Melli rushed back to the caramel tree where her friends huddled together. Raina was in the middle of the group with the Fairy Code Book on her lap. Melli hoped that while she had been with Cara the fairies had thought of a plan. This latest burst of butterscotch from the volcano had created even more trouble.

"We're in a hot butterscotch emergency," Melli cried as she flew up to the tree. "Now the spill is even deeper than before!"

"Take a breath," Cocoa told Melli. "We can't panic. We need to focus." She held out her hand to Melli. "Come sit down for a minute." She moved over to make room on the branch for her friend.

Melli knew Cocoa was right, but seeing more butterscotch flow from the volcano was upsetting. "It's getting worse down there," she said sadly.

"More butterscotch?" Dash asked. Her blue eyes were wide and full of fear.

"But we found something in the Fairy Code Book that might work," Raina said, giving Dash a stern look. "Remember, we have to remain calm." She held up the book to show Melli the picture. "We could build a barricade to block the butterscotch from spilling out into Chocolate Woods," Raina said slowly. "The idea is from this story about an overflow from Chocolate River."

"A barricade?" Melli said as she studied the picture.

"You see, Chocolate Fairies used bark and branches from a chocolate oak tree and tied them together, " Cocoa explained. "The bundle blocked the flow of chocolate coming from the rising river."

"The barricade saved Chocolate Woods," Berry added.

Melli bit her nails and looked up at her friends. "But butterscotch is much thicker and stickier than chocolate from Chocolate River. Will a chocolate barricade really work?"

Cocoa put her arm around Melli. "Chocolate Woods is so close. Let's get some chocolate branches and bark and give it a try."

"Chocolate is not the strongest material. It tends to flake," Dash pointed out.

Cocoa scowled at Dash. "We should at least try."

Melli turned to Dash. Everyone was feeling the pressure of the situation, and Melli didn't want her friends to fight. But Dash was a master at building sleds. She was one of the fastest racers in Sugar Valley and had even made her own sled and won a medal at the Marshmallow Run sled race. "Dash, do you have another suggestion?" Melli asked.

Dash looked down at the ground. "I don't know what would hold the syrup back," she said quietly. "Especially hot butterscotch."

The friends all glanced down at the spill.

"Cocoa is right," Melli said, breaking the silence. "Chocolate Woods is nearby and the easiest place for us to get materials. At least we can try to keep the spill from spreading so fast."

The fairies nodded in agreement. They flew off to the woods and gathered pieces of bark, twigs, and branches from the chocolate oaks. They put the materials on a large blanket, and each fairy took a corner. Melli flew in front to lead the way.

For the first time since she had seen the spill, Melli had a feeling of hope. Now if only this chocolate barricade would solve the problem!

Near the base of the volcano the five friends put the chocolate logs and bark on the ground. When the last of the wood was unloaded, Melli stood back and held her breath.

"Look!" she cried out. "The barricade is working!"

Butterscotch wasn't passing through the chocolate barricade. The five fairies joined hands and did a little dance. But their rejoicing didn't last long. After a few moments their feet were covered in the thick golden syrup.

Cocoa hung her head. "You were right, Dash," she said. "I'm sorry."

"We had to try," Dash said. "I'm really sorry that this didn't work. The chocolate wasn't strong or sticky enough to hold back the butterscotch."

Melli's wings fluttered and a smile appeared on her face. "Dash! That's it!" she exclaimed. Her feet lifted off the ground as she fluttered her wings. "That's the answer!" she shouted. Her friends stared at her, amazed at her outburst. "We need something that will be sticky and sturdy for sealing the crack," she said.

Raina, Cocoa, Dash, and Berry waited for Melli to explain.

"Bubble gum!" Melli finally exclaimed. She saw that her friends still didn't understand her idea. "If we can get enough sticky bubble gum, first we'll seal this crack, and then we'll be able to plug it up and stop the butterscotch from leaking!"

Raina considered Melli's plan. "I think you're on to something. Bubble gum would be an excellent choice. It's strong and sticky, and it would fill up the crack. But we'll need a lot of it."

"My cousin Pinkie makes bubble gum," Melli said enthusiastically. "She can help! She works at Candy Castle."

"Well then, let's go see her now!" Berry said.

Melli quickly wrote a sugar fly message to Cara explaining that she would be back shortly—

with another plan. Melli hoped this time their idea would work. Already there were too many birds harmed by the butterscotch spill.

"Let's hope this is a pink solution that will stick!" Melli said as she took the lead and flew toward Candy Castle.

5

Think Big

When the five fairies arrived at Candy Castle, there was a large group of fairies gathered in the Royal Gardens. The guards had just sounded their caramel horns, and Princess Lolli was standing on her balcony. The kind and gentle ruler was trying to quiet the crowd just as the fairies landed in the garden.

"Look!" Melli said. "We're just in time for Princess Lolli's announcement."

"Unfortunately, we've seen firsthand what is going on in Caramel Hills," Raina said. "I'm sure that is what she is going to talk about."

"Shh," Berry scolded. "She's ready to speak."

"Good afternoon," Princess Lolli said to the fairies in the Royal Gardens. "I know many of you have heard about the trouble in Caramel Hills. It is a very sad day." The princess looked around at the crowd. "There is a large crack near the base of the volcano, and hot butterscotch is leaking out into the hills."

Heavy sighs were heard throughout the crowd.

If only they could all see what is happening there now, Melli thought sadly.

 44

"The caramella birds that live up in the hills are in the greatest danger," Princess Lolli continued. "We need to work together to stop the spill and clean the animals that have been covered in the hot butterscotch."

"The news certainly has traveled fast," Cocoa said, looking around the Royal Gardens.

"We'll need everyone's help in the kingdom," Melli said. "I'm so glad to see so many fairies here."

"Sugar Valley is under a Kingdom Emergency," Princess Lolli declared. "All fairies are expected to help out in Caramel Hills. I hope to have more news for you soon." The princess turned to her right and waved her hand. Tula, one of Princess Lolli's advisers, appeared. "Tula will head the cleanup project. Please see her so we can get started as soon as possible."

The princess bowed her head and stepped back into the castle. Everyone felt her sadness. Princess Lolli was a good friend to all the creatures in Sugar Valley. Melli knew that this news was weighing heavily on her heart.

"Come," Melli said to her friends. "Let's go talk to Princess Lolli. I want to tell her about my plan."

The fairies flew into the castle. They waited patiently while the palace guard asked permission for them to enter the throne room. They found Princess Lolli near the window, looking out toward Caramel Hills.

"Princess Lolli, Caramel Hills is so awful," Melli blurted out. She ran up to the princess. "The caramella birds are trapped in the thick, hot butterscotch."

Princess Lolli gave Melli a tight hug. "I know," she said. "This is very disturbing news."

"But, Princess Lolli, we have a plan," Melli said, brightening. "A plan we think will work."

"At first we thought that if we could barricade the butterscotch, we could stop the leak, but that didn't work," Cocoa confessed. "The chocolate wood wasn't strong enough to hold the hot syrup."

"So instead, we thought we could seal the crack," Melli added.

Princess Lolli turned to face the five fairies before her. Her eyebrows shot up. "Tell me more," she said.

"My cousin Pinkie makes bubble gum here at the castle," Melli said. "If we can help her make enough sticky bubble gum, we might be able to mend the side of the volcano."

Princess Lolli smiled. "That is a fantastic idea," she said. "I am so impressed, and I'm grateful for your creative thinking." She walked over to her throne and sat down. "I think that is certainly worth a try!"

Melli was ready to burst with pride.

"Have you spoken to Pinkie?" Princess Lolli asked.

Melli shook her head. "We wanted to see what you thought about the idea first," she said.

Princess Lolli looked back out the window toward Caramel Hills. "Let's hope Pinkie can make enough gum."

"We'll help her," Melli offered.

"Thank you," Princess Lolli said. She called for one of the guards. "Please find Pinkie and ask her to come to the throne room at once." Then she faced Melli. "I must go speak to Tula before she leaves for Caramel Hills. You and your friends wait here for Pinkie. I'll be back shortly."

Melli and her friends looked at one another in amazement. They had been in Princess Lolli's throne room before, but they had never been there alone. They stood very still, not sure what to do.

Suddenly Melli began pacing around the room. "I hope Pinkie gets here soon."

"She'll be here," Cocoa told her. "Don't worry."

A short while later Pinkie flew into the throne room. She hugged Melli and her friends. She had heard about the Butterscotch Volcano disaster but had not realized how serious it had become. When Melli filled her in, her eyes started to brim with tears.

"And so we need to stop the leak in the

volcano," Melli said. "We thought your bubble gum could be the plug."

Pinkie tilted her head and flapped her pale pink wings. "I'm not sure I can do that," she said.

This was not the reply Melli had expected to hear. Her wings drooped down to the floor.

"I only make tiny pieces of bubble gum, Melli," Pinkie said. She dipped her hand into her pocket and pulled out three minia-ture gumballs.

Melli glanced up at her friends. Then her eyes settled on Princess Lolli's throne. The tall, wide peppermint sticks that Dash had created for the princess made the throne extra-special.

Melli thought back to when Dash had been growing the peppermint sticks for the princess's new throne and training for the Marshmallow Run. No one had believed that Dash could both manage her training and create the large royal peppermints, but she had. Melli moved closer to Dash.

"When you were making the peppermint sticks for the throne, they were the biggest sticks you had ever made, right?" Melli asked.

Dash nodded. She reached into her bag for a snack.

"Did you do anything differently?" Melli asked.

Taking a nibble of her treat, Dash shook her head. "Not really," she said.

"They took longer to grow, but those sticks are the same as the small ones right here." Dash showed off a smaller peppermint stick in her hand.

"And I bet those taste the same," Cocoa said, smiling. She winked at Melli. She knew exactly what her clever friend was doing.

"Sure as sugar!" Dash exclaimed.

"You see, Pinkie," Melli said, jumping up, "it's still the same bubble gum. You just have to make much, much, much more."

"We can help you create the most bubble gum ever," Raina said. "You can do this, Pinkie!"

"We're all counting on you," Melli told her.

Pinkie looked concerned, but Melli hoped Dash's peppermint sticks would inspire her cousin—and change her mind.

CHAPTER
6

A Sugar-tastic Idea

Melli's wings twitched as she waited to hear Pinkie's reply. She hoped her cousin would agree to make a superbig bubble gum plug for the volcano. Waiting for her to answer was so hard! She crossed her fingers. Then she listened to her four friends, who surrounded Pinkie.

"We're asking for your help for all the cara-mella birds in Caramel Hills," Cocoa said.

Melli shot her friend Cocoa a grateful look.

"Maybe if you went to Caramel Hills and saw the problem close-up, you'd understand why we desperately need your help," Raina said. "You could see what your bubble gum will do."

Melli was thankful for Raina's calm and thoughtful response. And it seemed to help Pinkie with her decision.

The small Bubble Gum Fairy fluttered her wings. She raised her eyebrows and let out a deep breath. "Will you all come with me?" she asked.

"Sure as sugar!" the five friends said in unison.

The fairies flew out of Candy Castle and

across the kingdom to Caramel Hills. As they flew along Chocolate River, Melli glanced over at Pinkie.

"I know this seems crazy to you," Melli said. "But I really think bubble gum is the answer."

Pinkie nodded. "I need to see the problem before I try to make a solution," she said.

Melli understood. She hoped that when Pinkie saw the cracked volcano, she'd realize why bubble gum was their best shot at fixing the leak. She led Pinkie and her friends straight to Butterscotch Volcano. At the bottom of the volcano Melli spotted Cara and flew down to greet her.

"I'm so glad you're back," Cara blurted out. "The butterscotch is spreading fast—and heading dangerously close to Chocolate Woods."

"It would be a disastrous and delicious mess in Chocolate Woods," Dash said with a wistful look in her eyes.

Melli knew that Dash often thought with her stomach first. She smiled at her, knowing that she meant no harm.

"We brought Pinkie here because we're hoping she can make a bubble gum seal for the leak in the volcano," Melli told her. She turned around and saw Pinkie with her mouth gaping open.

"This is awful," Pinkie said softly. "Show me the crack."

Taking her hand, Melli and Pinkie left the butterscotch-covered ground and flew up to the side of the volcano to take a closer look at the leak.

 57

"Here it is," Melli said, pointing. "You can see how the butterscotch is pooling on the flat land."

Pinkie stared at the volcano for a minute. "Wow, that's a mighty big crack."

"Do you think you can make enough bubble gum for us, Pinkie?" Melli asked. She knew seeing the sticky situation firsthand had made her want to help.

"I am going to try my hardest," Pinkie told her. "I'll need more time and some extra Candy Fairy help."

"Take Berry and Raina with you," Melli said. "They will be excellent helpers. Dash, Cocoa, and I will stay here with Cara."

"That sounds like a perfect pink plan," Pinkie said. "Let's meet back here before Sun Dip."

Melli hugged Pinkie. "Thank you," she said.

"I'll see you later." Then she smiled at her cousin. "Good luck!"

While Berry, Raina, and Pinkie returned to Candy Castle, Cocoa, Dash, and Melli went to see how they could help Cara.

"Tula just dropped off more supplies," Cara said. She pointed to a few boxes lying on the ground.

"I can unpack and organize those things," Cocoa offered.

"I'll start cleaning these little birds over here, okay, Cara?" Melli asked.

"They've been waiting a long time," Cara said. "They'll be glad to be butterscotch-free."

For the next few hours the fairies worked hard washing caramella birds of every shape and size. When the birds were free of butterscotch,

they swooped through the air, happy to fly once again.

"I've cleaned so many birds, but there are still more who are covered in this goo," Melli told her friends.

"It's a butterscotch disaster, all right," Dash sighed. Then she bent down to dip her finger in the thick butterscotch pool. "But I have to admit, this syrup is *really* delicious," she said, licking her finger.

"Leave it to Dash to still have an appetite even during a full-on Candy Kingdom emergency," Cocoa said. She crossed her arms across her chest.

For the first time since Melli had spotted the first butterscotch-coated bird, she laughed.

Dash's stomach was reliable—she was hungry all the time!

"I'm serious," Dash said, blushing.

Cocoa started to laugh. "I know you are," she said, smiling. "Believe me, I wish I could use all this good butterscotch. What a waste."

Melli's face lit up. "Hot caramel!" she screamed.

Dash and Cocoa looked at her. "What happened?" they said at the same time.

Fluttering her wings excitedly, Melli flew up in the air. "Nothing happened," she explained. "Except that you both gave me a *sugar-tastic* idea!" When she saw that her friends still looked confused, she said, "The butterscotch is delicious, and it is a shame that fairies can't use the syrup. This is an awful waste."

"Why is she saying what we already know?" Dash whispered to Cocoa.

"Because you're right!" Melli exclaimed. "We need to store and save the butterscotch. Let's get those big barrels from Candy Castle here and fill them with butterscotch."

"*Sweeeeet!*" Dash cheered.

"Maybe that would lower the level of the syrup pool here too," Cocoa said. "Look how high the butterscotch is now."

Dash held up her hand. "Wait a minty minute. *How* are we going to get the syrup into the barrels? And how are we going to get the barrels from the castle here to Caramel Hills?"

Melli sighed. "I didn't think of that. Any ideas?"

"Where's Raina with her Fairy Code Book when you need her?" Cocoa said with a sigh.

63

Melli thought back to the last Butterscotch Festival. She remembered there were tubes set up from the volcano that led to the caramel barrels. "We need tubes," she said. "Something to pour the syrup in and move it from one place to another." She turned to Dash. "What would you make a tube out of?"

Dash thought for a moment. She snapped her fingers. "Toffee," she called out. "It's strong and slippery. I think toffee candy will be perfect."

Melli gave Dash a hug. "Sure as sugar, this is going to work! Dash, you get the toffee, and Cocoa and I will get the barrels."

"So mint!" Dash said. "I know just the toffee tree to visit for a good strong piece. It might take me a while to carve out a tube, but I'll try."

"Dash," Melli said, "I'm sure you'll do a

 64

sugar-tastic job! We'll meet you back here before Sun Dip."

Feeling a burst of energy, Melli and Cocoa flew back to Candy Castle. Melli knew they'd find a large barrel there for them to take back to hold the butterscotch. Now all the syrup would not go to waste. And maybe, just maybe, they could stop the spill from spreading all over Sugar Valley.

CHAPTER
7

Supersweet

At Candy Castle there were fairies flying busily around. With the kingdom in a state of emergency, everyone in Sugar Valley was helping out. So many fairies cared about Caramel Hills.

"There's Tula," Melli said. "Cocoa, let's ask her about finding some empty barrels. I'm sure she can help us."

The two fairies flew over to Tula, who was surrounded by a large group of fairies. She had a scroll and a long feather pen in her hands.

"Lemona, please take your crew of Sour Orchard Fairies to the animal rescue center set up in Caramel Hills," Tula said. "You'll find Cara the Caramel Fairy there, and she will advise you."

Melli's heart swelled with pride. She wanted to shout, "That's my little sister!" She watched as the group of Sour Orchard Fairies flew off. Berry was friends with Lemona. One time Berry had even gone to Sour Orchard, and Lemona had been very nice to her. Once again Melli was touched that so many fairies wanted to help.

"We're next," Cocoa said, pulling Melli closer to Tula.

Tula didn't even look up from her scroll. Melli wasn't sure if she should speak first. She looked over at Cocoa, who nodded toward Tula.

"Go ahead," Cocoa urged her friend. "Tell her your plan."

Melli cleared her throat. She suddenly felt as if her voice would not come out. She took a deep breath. "Tula," she said, "we have an idea about storing the overflow of butterscotch from the volcano."

Tula peered over her sugarcoated glasses at the two young fairies in front of her.

Cocoa squeezed Melli's hand, encouraging her to go on.

"You see, the extra butterscotch is causing so much trouble," Melli said quickly. "If we can get some of the syrup into barrels like we did at the

Butterscotch Festival, we could stop the overflow and save the butterscotch syrup for later." Melli waited as Tula turned her gaze on her.

"Your name is Melli, right?" Tula said, staring at her.

"Yes," Melli said quietly. She stood perfectly still. She hoped that Tula thought she had a good idea.

"Melli," Tula said. She took off her glasses and looked into Melli's eyes. "Not one other fairy here has come up with such a good suggestion."

Melli looked down at her feet and fluttered her wings.

"Princess Lolli is not here," Tula went on. "She is at Butterscotch Volcano. But I think that is a supersweet idea. I like when a fairy is thinking! We'll have to get some of the palace guards to carry the large barrels over to Caramel Hills. Will you fly with them and direct the project?"

"Sure as sugar!" Melli replied. "I would be happy to show them where to go."

"Let me speak to the guards, and you can meet them out by the Royal Gardens," Tula said. "Give me about ten minutes."

"Thank you!" Melli said, bursting with pride.

Cocoa pulled Melli's hand. "While we're waiting, let's see how Pinkie is doing," she said.

Melli and Cocoa flew over to the bubble gum garden, just outside the Royal Gardens gate. In the middle of the garden Melli saw Berry, Raina, and Pinkie standing over a wide barrel.

"How is everything going?" Melli asked as she landed next to Pinkie. She looked into the bowl and saw a mound of pink gum.

Pinkie pulled the long paddle out of the barrel. Stretching her arm up high, she showed off the fresh batch of bubble gum. "Berry and Raina have helped me so much," she said. "With their encouragement and their sweet ways, I think we've made the largest wad of bubble gum ever!"

The pink sticky candy looked good enough to eat—and sticky enough to plug up a crack. "I think you're right!" Melli exclaimed. She clapped her hands together.

Cocoa filled them in on the plan with the barrels and Dash's project of building a tube for the butterscotch syrup.

"Good thinking," Raina said.

Melli blushed. "I remembered a chapter in the Fairy Code Book about the Butterscotch Festival," she said.

Raina's eyes sparkled. "Ah, you did!" she said. "Lickin' lollipops!"

"We need to make some more bubble gum," Pinkie told her cousin. "That volcano crack was very wide and deep. We should probably make another batch this size."

Melli agreed. "We still have a little more time before Sun Dip," she said. "Cocoa and I are going to fly back to Caramel Hills with the barrels. Will you meet us there?"

"Yes," Pinkie said. "Before Sun Dip for sure— just as we planned."

"You'll need some guards to fly this gum over to Caramel Hills," Melli told her friends. "There's no way you'll be able to pick up this barrel!"

Raina laughed. "We already spoke to Tula

about getting guards to help us," she said. "Don't worry. We'll see you later."

Melli and Cocoa and four palace guards flew back to the volcano with four large barrels. The barrels might not hold all the overflowing butter-scotch, but it was a start. And that was the best she could hope for right now.

CHAPTER 8

A Sticky Plan

Back at Caramel Hills there was a swarm of fairies flying near the volcano. Melli's heart started to pound.

"Maybe something awful has happened while we were at Candy Castle," she said to Cocoa. She tried to see the volcano, but there were too many fairies in the way. "I can't see a thing!" she cried. "Do you think the volcano erupted? Oh, that would be awful! Then there'd be even more butterscotch flowing over Caramel Hills."

Cocoa shook her head. "Just calm down," she said. "If Berry were here, she'd tell you not to dip your wings in syrup yet." Flapping her wings, Cocoa leaped higher in the air and squinted her eyes.

"Do you see anything?" Melli called up to her. She couldn't bear the thought of more syrup rushing over the hills.

"Nothing happened, I think!" Cocoa shouted. "Come up here. I see Princess Lolli." She pointed to the center of the crowd. "There are a bunch of castle guards surrounding her. She must be here to see the volcano firsthand."

Melli flew up next to Cocoa. It was easy to

 77

spot Princess Lolli's strawberry-blond hair and her sugarcoated sparkly tiara. She was examining the crack and the damage done by the hot, sticky syrup.

"I want to tell her about our plan with the barrels," Melli said. "I'm sure she'll be pleased." She darted quickly in and out of the crowd to where Princess Lolli was talking to one of her advisers.

"Princess Lolli," Melli called. She waved and flew close to her.

"Hello, Melli," Princess Lolli said. "How is Pinkie coming along with the bubble gum? We will need a very big wad of gum to plug this crack."

"She's working on it," Melli informed her. "Berry and Raina are helping out." She took a deep breath. She was so anxious to tell Princess Lolli her idea about saving some of the overflowing butterscotch that she was having trouble breathing!

Princess Lolli put a hand on her back. "What is it, Melli?" she said kindly. "Is there something more?"

"Yes," Melli said. "Cocoa and I have another idea that might save the butterscotch and stop some of the overflow. We spoke to Tula about the plan. Would you like to hear it?"

Princess Lolli's eyes widened. "I'd love to hear some good news, or at least a good idea right about now," she said.

Melli explained the plan while Cocoa showed

 79

the castle guards where to put the barrels.

"We thought if we could capture some of the butterscotch, the spill wouldn't get wider," Melli told the princess.

Princess Lolli's wings fluttered. "This is a fine idea," she said, "but how will we get the butter-scotch into the barrels?"

Dash flew up behind the princess and Melli with a long, narrow toffee tube in her arms. "With this!" she cried. "We can stick it in the crack and seal the gum around the tube. Then all the butterscotch will flow through it and into the barrel."

Princess Lolli examined the tube. A smile spread across her face. "Sure as sugar, it's worth a try!" she declared.

"The bubble gum should be ready before Sun

Dip," Melli said. She looked up to the sky. It would be a little longer before the sun touched the tips of the Frosted Mountains.

"We'll have to be patient," Princess Lolli said, seeing disappointment in Melli's face. "I'm going to check in with the rescue center. Keep an eye out for Pinkie and the others. Send for me when they arrive so we can all be a part of Bubble Gum Rescue."

Melli watched Princess Lolli as she flew away from the volcano and back down to the animal rescue center. Normally, the princess had a lovely smile on her face. But today, Melli noticed, there was a deep crease in her forehead and she looked very troubled. She knew that seeing all the animals in danger broke the princess's heart.

"We need the bubble gum now," Melli said.

"Don't worry," Cocoa said. She was back from helping the guards with the barrels. "Pinkie will come. For now we should go help at the animal rescue center, don't you think?"

Melli followed Cocoa down to the base of the volcano and joined the other fairies. Working together made the task go faster, and time moved quickly.

After Melli finished washing her fifth caramella bird, she glanced up at the sky. The sun was nearing the tip of the Frosted Mountains.

Where is Pinkie? She has to get here! Melli thought.

Cocoa could see that her friend was worrying more and more. "Let's go back up to the volcano," Cocoa said to Melli. "They should be back soon."

Together, the two fairies hovered in the sky,

and just then Melli saw Berry, Raina, Dash, and Pinkie flying toward the volcano. Behind them were four palace guards holding the two large barrels of pink bubble gum.

"We've got bubble gum!" Berry announced as she drew closer. "Bubble Gum Rescue is ready to begin!"

"That is sweet news to hear on this dreadfully gooey day," Melli called. She flew up to Pinkie and gave her a hug. "I knew you could do this!" she cried.

"Pinkie whipped up the biggest and the stickiest bubble gum batch ever," Raina added.

"And I wouldn't have been able to do it without Berry and Raina's help," Pinkie told her cousin.

"Cocoa, go get Princess Lolli," Melli said. "Tell her we're ready to start the rescue!"

"I'll be back in a flash," Cocoa said, speeding down to the bottom of the volcano.

"Pinkie, all this bubble gum is fantastic!" Melli said. She peered into the barrel. "This just has to work!" she cried.

"I hope so," Pinkie said. She couldn't take her eyes off the large crack in the side of the mountain.

"Bubble Gum Rescue will work," Melli said. "You'll see."

She crossed her fingers and hoped that her prediction would come true.

CHAPTER

9

Pink and Positive

Melli and her friends hovered near the crack on the side of Butterscotch Volcano, waiting for Cocoa to return with Princess Lolli. *Oh, please hurry,* Melli thought as she kept watch for Cocoa and the fairy princess.

"What happens if there isn't enough bubble gum?" Pinkie asked as she hovered beside Melli.

"That crack is so deep. I'm not sure we've made enough to patch it up." Pinkie's pale pink wings were beating quickly, and her forehead was wrinkled with worry.

Melli was concerned too. She looked over at Berry and Raina, who were bobbing up and down in the wind. If only she could be as calm as her friends!

"Don't worry, Pinkie," Melli managed to say. "Whatever you made will help. Let's try to think positive."

Pinkie nodded. "I'll try," she said. "Pink and positive," she muttered over and over.

When Melli spotted Cocoa and Princess Lolli, she waved both her arms in the air and called out to them. "Over here! Oh, sweet sugar, they're finally here."

Cocoa waved back, and the two fairies flew toward them.

"Hello," Princess Lolli said, greeting the fairies. "Cocoa said that the bubble gum is ready. This is certainly sweet news."

"Yes," Pinkie said. "But we need help. The barrels of bubble gum are too heavy. We can't lift them."

"The guards are here to assist you," Princess Lolli said. She flew over and peered into one of the containers. "This is very fine work," she called. "Thank you." She smiled at Pinkie, Berry, and Raina.

"Let Bubble Gum Rescue begin!" Princess Lolli declared.

Then she turned to one of the castle guards. "Let's spread the gum around and see if we can seal the crack."

In a flash the guards moved the barrels closer to the volcano.

Dash took the long toffee tube she had cradled in her arms up to the crack. "I hope this works," she said. "We'll all need to hold the tube in place while the guards pour the bubble gum."

Melli saw Pinkie's confused expression, so she explained Dash's plan.

"We have some yummy ideas for all that butterscotch," Dash whispered to Pinkie.

Princess Lolli regarded the toffee tube. "This is *so mint*, Dash," she said with a smile.

Melli glanced over at Dash. She saw her minty friend blushing to the shade of red in a candy cane. "Thank you," she said.

"Oh, peppermint sticks!" Dash exclaimed. "It was the least I could do. I couldn't stand to see all that butterscotch wasted." She leaned in closer to Melli. "Promise me a special butterscotch candy later?"

Laughing, Melli hugged Dash. "Bubbling butterscotch, you've got yourself a deal!" she cried.

The Candy Castle guards poured the bubble gum from the barrels. With long, heavy paddles, they spread the sticky mixture into the crack.

Melli and her friends grabbed one end of the tube, holding it in the crack as the guards filled bubble gum in around it.

"All right," one of the guards called. "You can let go. The tube is secure."

The five fairies held their breath and flew up in the air.

"I don't know if I can look," said Cocoa.

"Yes, you can! Open your eyes, Cocoa. It's a sweet surprise!" said Melli.

No more butterscotch was leaking out of the volcano's side! Instead, a steady stream of the golden syrup was pouring out of the tube—and into a large barrel off to the side.

"Hot butterscotch!" Melli cheered.

"We did it!" Cocoa shouted.

A roar of applause rose up in Caramel Hills. All the fairies rejoiced and sang out. Bubble Gum Rescue was a huge success!

Melli rushed over to Pinkie. "Thank you," she said. "I knew you could do this."

Pinkie squeezed her cousin tight. "I never would have thought of this idea. Thank you for dreaming it up." She turned to face Berry and Raina. "And thank you, too!"

 92

"We were happy to lend some sugar," Raina said, grinning.

"Sweet strawberries," Berry said, coming up to Pinkie. "You did all the work, Pinkie. You should be extra-proud."

This was a time to celebrate, but Melli couldn't stop thinking of the caramella birds at the base of the volcano. There were still many suffering because of the butterscotch spill.

"What's wrong, Melli?" Cocoa asked. "You don't look happy. You should be! We just stopped the gushing butterscotch—and even managed to save the syrup."

Melli looked down at her feet. "I know," she said softly. She couldn't even speak about the awful thought that had popped into her head. "But . . ." She couldn't get the words out.

 93

Raina flew up next to her. "Are you worried about the caramella birds?" she asked. "Why don't we check in on the rescue center now?"

Melli hoped the animals in the center would be all right—especially if all the Candy Fairies continued to help. But that was not the only thing bothering her.

"Tell us," Cocoa said. "Please."

Melli bit her nails. "It's just . . ." She knew she had to say the words quickly, otherwise she wouldn't be able to tell her friends. Melli took a deep breath. She started to explain. "Now the crack is sealed and the gushing butterscotch syrup stopped." She paused and looked at the concerned faces surrounding her. "But what if this happens again?" Melli asked, her voice trembling. She watched her friends' expressions.

Each Candy Fairy had the same sad look. They were thinking the same sour thought.

None of them could have predicted what had happened in Caramel Hills. And they wouldn't be able to prevent the volcano from cracking or erupting.

Melli looked to each of her friends. But she knew that none of them had a magic answer for her.

10

Bubbles of Happiness

Melli's question hung in the air. None of the fairies knew how to respond. Luckily, Princess Lolli was close enough to hear the question, and she immediately flew to the fairies.

"Melli, you asked a very good question," Princess Lolli told her. "There are many events we can be prepared for in Sugar Valley. We can try to prevent sour things from happening, but there is much we can't predict or prevent." She motioned for the fairies to move closer. When the fairies were huddled together, she continued. "Sadly, many events that happen are out of our control."

"Like a volcano leaking," Melli said.

"Or a river overflowing," Cocoa added.

"Even a rainstorm," Raina said softly.

"Yes, there are many things that happen naturally here in the valley," Princess Lolli said. "But working together can make life sweeter and safer. All the fairies in the kingdom should feel very proud for lending a helping hand."

Raina took the Fairy Code Book from her bag and showed the first page. "That's what the Fairy Code Book says too." She read, "'Nature can't

always be predicted, so take care and be aware.'"

Princess Lolli nodded. "We all need to watch out for one another . . . and keep an eye out for leaking volcanoes!"

All of a sudden Cara came racing up to the group. "Please, come quick!" she cried.

"What's happened?" Melli asked. Cara looked upset, and Melli worried one of the caramella birds might be seriously injured.

"Please," Cara begged. "Come now!"

The fairies raced quickly to the animal rescue center. Melli could hardly breathe she was so nervous.

But once there Melli found quite a sight. Instead of finding a seriously wounded caramella, she saw a group of birds happy and clean.

"The caramella birds want to thank you all for your clever work," Cara said proudly. "I was bursting to tell you, but I promised that I would make this a surprise."

Melli hugged her little sister. "You've been pure as sugar," she said. "Thank you for helping so much with the rescue center."

"This is the sweetest part of the day," Cara said, hugging her sister. "I'm so glad that Caramel Hills is almost back to normal.

"With extra butterscotch!" Dash blurted out.

She looked around at the barrels of butterscotch that had already been filled. "It's like the Butterscotch Festival has come early this year."

"Dash, that is an excellent idea," Princess Lolli said, smiling. "Why not have a celebration now? All the fairies worked so hard to rescue the caramellas and save Caramel Hills. I think we should have a party!"

"A bubblicious party!" Pinkie exclaimed.

"I couldn't think of anything more fitting for this occasion," the princess proclaimed.

With a declaration from Princess Lolli, the fairies started to fly . . . and soon the rescue center had been turned into a place fit for a royal celebration.

Pinkie, Berry, and Raina were a *sugar-ific* team again and created delicious bubble gum bubbles.

"A rainbow of bubbles," Melli said when she saw the colorful decorations. "A sweet touch since the whole rescue mission was made possible by bubble gum!"

Cocoa and Melli joined several other Candy Fairies to whip up butterscotch candies.

"I'm so happy this butterscotch didn't go to waste," Cocoa said as she arranged the trays of freshly made candies.

Dash popped a candy into her mouth. "Mmm, you can say that again," she said, licking her lips.

Everyone in Sugar Valley was enjoying the festivities in Caramel Hills. "Nothing like a delicious turn of events," Melli whispered to Raina.

"How sweet it is," she agreed.

A caramella bird landed on Melli's shoulder and nuzzled her neck.

"Hey, little sweets," Melli said, recognizing the yellow bird. "Weren't you covered in butterscotch the last time I saw you?" She rubbed the bird's neck and listened to the soft cooing. "I'm glad you are feeling better," she said. "Now let's try to keep you clean—and safe!"

The bird flew off into Caramel Hills. Melli smiled. She watched her friends enjoying Sun Dip in Caramel Hills. She felt relieved that once again her home was clean.

The quiet and still Butterscotch Volcano stood behind her. She eyed the bubble gum patch on the side. Princess Lolli was right: There was no way to predict another crack or sticky spill. But Melli knew her fairy friends would always be there for her—and the animals. Sure as sugar, Sugar Valley would stick—and work—together.

And that made Melli feel extra-thankful.

"Melli!" Cocoa called. "Everyone is loving our caramel chocolate rolls."

"It feels like ages since we made those," Melli said. "What a long day!"

Cocoa smiled. "Come on, you must try this *butterscotch* hot chocolate. It's double delicious!"

Melli flew over to where her friends and Cara were sitting. She took a cup and Cocoa poured her a serving of the hot, yummy drink. Then Melli raised her cup high in the air. "Here's a toast to bubble gum and to the best team of Candy Fairies!" she said.

The fairies cheered, and everyone enjoyed the sweet drink as the sun settled down behind the Frosted Mountains.

Double Dip

For Rachel, who discovered the healing power
of mint ice cream sandwiches!

1

Master of Mint

The sweet smell of peppermint made Dash's silver wings flutter. The small Mint Fairy was tending to her candies in Peppermint Grove. The weather was turning a little cooler, and there were many mint candies sprouting on the vines. This was perfect mint-chip weather! Dash picked a tiny mint pod from a stem in front of her. Carefully, she opened up the green pod, plucked the tiny mint chips out, and popped them into her mouth. "Mmm," she said. "Just right!"

"How are the new chips?" asked Minny. The young Mint Fairy flew over to Dash. "I've been waiting for those to ripen. How do they taste?"

"Perfect," Dash reported happily. She handed a pod to Minny. "Let me know what you think."

Minny put a handful of chips in her mouth and quickly agreed. "Yum, these are good," she said. "Dash, you are the master of mint!"

Dash blushed. She was excited about the mini mint chips. She thought they'd be perfect toppings for chocolates or even for ice cream. Just thinking about the yummy treats made her stomach rumble.

"Maybe we should take a break for lunch," Dash suggested. She rubbed her belly. "I'm starving."

Minny laughed. "Dash, you are always hungry!"

Dash couldn't argue. "I might be small, but I do have a huge appetite!" she said, laughing.

There wasn't a candy in Sugar Valley that Dash didn't love . . . although some she liked more than others!

The two Mint Fairies settled down under the shade of a few large peppermint leaves. Dash was thankful for the rest—and the delicious fruit nectar that she had brought for lunch.

"Oh, look, Dash!" Minny exclaimed. "There's a sugar fly note for you." She pointed to the fly circling over Dash's head.

Sugar flies brought messages to fairies throughout Sugar Valley. The flies could spread information—or gossip— to fairies far and wide. Dash quickly opened the note and then flew straight up in the air.

"Holy peppermint!" she cried. She zoomed around and then did a somersault.

"What did that note say?" Minny asked. She leaped up in excitement. "Must be extra-sweet news."

Dash flew back down to the ground. "I just got the best invitation," she told her friend. "You will not believe this. *I* can't believe this!" She shot up in the air again.

"What?" Minny begged. "Come down and tell me!"

"This is *so mint*!" Dash gushed. "Wait till all my friends hear about this!" She scribbled off a note and handed it back to the sugar fly. "Please take this back to Meringue Island as fast as possible," Dash instructed. "My answer is YES!"

Minny's eyes grew wide. "Meringue Island?" she said. "Why, that's all the way in the Vanilla Sea!"

"Yes," Dash said. "And right near Mt. Ice Cream."

Clapping her hands, Minny cheered. "I know— were you invited to race in Double Dip?" she shouted.

"Sure as sugar!" Dash said, flipping in the air again.

"Dash, that is minty cool!" Minny exclaimed. "I've only read about that race. And now you are going to be in it!"

"I can't believe it," Dash repeated, landing back down on the ground.

Minny sighed. "I've never been all the way to Meringue Island," she said wistfully. "I've heard that the Cone Harbor Festival weekend is supersweet. They have all these amazing flavors of ice cream and candy toppings for fairies to taste, and lots of carnival rides and parties." She blushed when Dash raised her eyebrows. "I read all about the festival in the *Daily Scoop*," she confessed.

Dash smiled. "I know. I've read those articles too! The festival seems totally mint," she said. "And I've heard the Double Dip course is one of the most challenging sled races. The race is the last day of the festival."

"Does that mean you'll have to race against Menta and Peppa?" Minny asked. "They've been the champions for the past two years."

"So you know about those Mint Fairies?" Dash said, raising her eyebrows. "They make mint ice cream and live on Meringue Island. They definitely have an advantage because they've run the course so many times. But this year the race is going to be different."

"Why?" Minny asked, taking a sip of her drink.

"Because this year *I'm* in the race!" Dash boasted proudly. "I've never been to Mt. Ice Cream. But now that I've been invited to go, I can't wait! It's not every day that a fairy gets invited to race in Double Dip!" Dash's mind started to flood with ideas. "I can't wait to start working on a new sled. I'll need a double sled for this race," she explained. "And I know just the partner to pick to ride with me."

"Who?" Minny asked. She leaned in closer to Dash.

"The perfect fairy for the job," she said. "She's fearless, and she knows chocolate inside and out."

"Oh, I've read there is that chocolate-coated part of the course," Minny said. She tapped her finger on her head. "I've heard that is the part where lots of fairies fall off their sleds."

"Exactly!" Dash exclaimed. "So with my secret chocolate partner, I'll have the winning edge."

"And a good friend to race with," Minny said,

giggling. "I know you are talking about your friend Cocoa. She'll be fantastic."

Taking a bite of a mint, Dash nodded in agreement. "I hope that she agrees. We'd make a *sugar-tastic* team."

Dash called over another sugar fly. "I wonder if Carobee the dragon would take my friends and me to Meringue Island. The journey would be so sweet on top of a dragon! I hope he will agree to fly us across the Vanilla Sea." She wrote her note and handed it to the sugar fly. "You'll find Carobee in the caves on Meringue Island," Dash told the fly. "Please hurry, and wait for his reply!"

Dash imagined the green-and-purple dragon getting the sugar fly note. She and her friends had met Carobee when they'd been searching for gooey goblins. While they had been looking for the mischievous creatures, they'd found Carobee. The fairies had become fast friends with the dragon after that adventure. Dash hoped that Carobee would be part of this adventure too!

The fly buzzed off toward Meringue Island. Dash leaned back and took a deep, slow breath in and out. "I just know this is going to be my year to win," she said. "To win Double Dip is a huge honor."

"And to beat Menta and Peppa would be a great accomplishment," Minny added.

"Hmm," Dash said, closing her eyes, thinking about the moment of glory. "Can't you see Cocoa and me in the winner's circle?" She sighed. "This is going to be *so mint*!" she exclaimed. "But first I have to ask Cocoa to be my partner!"

CHAPTER

2

Sweet News

The sun was near the top of the Frosted Mountains when Dash arrived at Red Licorice Lake. She knew she was early for Sun Dip, but she was too excited—and maybe a little worried. Cocoa, her Chocolate Fairy friend, would be the best partner for her. But would she say yes to the race?

Dash knew that Cocoa liked adventures. She was a spunky fairy who had once stood up to Mogu the salty troll. He had stolen Cocoa's chocolate eggs, and she had gone all the way to Black Licorice Swamp to get them back. Cocoa was brave and clever. Even though Cocoa had never raced before, Dash knew that she had what it took to be a great speed racer.

Sitting down on the red sugar sand, Dash thought about what she would say to Cocoa. She spoke aloud, "Cocoa, I have the mintiest, most exciting quest . . . *Ach-hoo! Ach-hoo! Ach-hoo!*" Dash started sneezing, and then sniffled.

"Dash, are you all right?" Raina the Gummy Fairy asked as she landed next to her friend.

"Oh, yes, I'm fine," Dash said. "Nothing a little mint won't cure!" She reached into her pocket and showed off her new mint candy.

Raina smiled. "Your mint chips!" she exclaimed. "Those look delicious."

"And they taste good too," Dash said, grinning. "Try them." She poured some into Raina's hand.

"Mmm," Raina said. "Well done, Dash!"

"And that isn't the mint news of the day," Dash informed her.

"Tell me!" Raina said, moving closer.

Dash straightened up. She had planned on keeping her news a secret until all her friends had arrived, but she couldn't keep quiet any longer. She pulled her wings back and smiled at Raina. "I was invited to race in Double Dip!" she exclaimed.

Raina jumped up in the air. "Licking lollipops, Dash! That is *sugar-tastic*!"

"Do you think Cocoa will want to be my sledding partner?" Dash asked.

"Cocoa is one of the most fearless fairies," Raina said thoughtfully. "She could definitely help you out on the chocolate slope of the Double Dip course."

Dash flapped her wings enthusiastically. "Exactly. Plus, it sure would be so mint to race with a good friend." She looked at Raina. "Do you think that she'll say yes?"

"It's not even Sun Dip, and you are already eating and telling stories," Melli the Caramel Fairy said, interrupting their conversation. She smiled at her friends as she touched down on the ground.

Cocoa was right behind Melli. "Leave it to Dash to be early," she said. "And eating," she joked as she pointed to Dash's mint chips.

Raina laughed. "Something has gotten Dash all juiced up," she said. She faced Dash. "Tell them!" she whispered.

Dash grinned, and her silver wings fluttered. "Let's wait until Berry arrives," she said. "I want to share my news when everyone is here."

"That's not fair," Cocoa moaned. "You know Berry is *always* late."

Melli spread a blanket, and the four fairies sat

 123

down. Dash saw that the sun was inching closer to the top of the mountains. She looked over toward Fruit Chew Meadow.

Please hurry, Berry! Dash thought. *For once, make it on time!*

Raina gave Dash a look. Dash wanted to ask Cocoa right then, but she thought it would be sweeter if all the fairies were together. She tapped her fingers on her knees. If Berry didn't arrive soon, Dash thought for sure she would burst!

"Ach-hoo! Ach-hoo! Ach-hoo!" Dash sneezed again. She noticed her friends sharing a look. "I'm fine," she told them. "Just some licorice pollen in the air, I'm sure."

Raina raised her eyebrows, but Dash jumped up and cut her off before she could say anything

 124

more. "There's Berry!" Dash cried, pointing up to the sky.

Berry floated down to her friends. The Fruit Fairy's red-and-pink dress was sparkling, and in her hair she wore matching sugarcoated barrettes. Berry loved fashion and was definitely the best-dressed fairy of the friends. Part of the reason she was often late was that she spent so much time getting ready.

"Hi, everyone!" Berry said. "Wait until you hear!" She grinned at all her friends. "I have the most delicious news!"

Raina put her hand up. "I don't know, Berry," she said, "Dash has something supersweet to share." She pushed Dash into the middle of the fairies.

"Tell us, Dash!" Melli said.

Dash grinned. "I was invited to be in the Double Dip race at Mt. Ice Cream during the Cone Harbor Festival!" she blurted out. She felt her cheeks flush with color as the excitement bubbled up inside her.

"Congratulations!" her friends all cheered.

"Wow," Melli said. "That is a great honor."

"Sweet strawberries," Berry said.

"I have another surprise, Cocoa," Dash said, turning to her. "I would love if you'd be my partner on the sled. Double Dip is a two-fairy race. I'd be honored if you'd race with me."

Cocoa's eyes sparkled. "One hundred and fifty cocoa percent!" she shouted. She shot up in the air and did a flip. "A race on Mt. Ice Cream? *Choc-o-licious*!"

"And Carobee is going to take us!" Dash said. "I sent a sugar fly message to him, and he wrote back right away. He can't wait to visit with us again."

"Sure as sugar, this is going to be such a great trip," Berry said. She grinned. "Your news is the icing on my news, Dash."

"What are you talking about?" Raina asked, eyeing her clever friend.

Berry stood up. "My delicious news is that Fruli has invited us all to stay at her place on Meringue Island for the Cone Harbor Festival weekend!"

"So mint!" Dash cheered. "Now we have a grand place to stay! Double Dip is the last event in the festival. This is scrumptious!"

"Fruli said we could all come?" Melli asked.

Berry nodded. "Yes, and that was before Dash and Cocoa were going to race! Now it's all even sweeter."

Fruli was a fancy Fruit Fairy from Meringue Island. She worked in Fruit Chew Meadow with Berry. There was a time when Berry had been very jealous of her, but now they were good friends.

Dash glanced up at the Frosted Mountains. The sun was nestled behind the high white peaks. She couldn't wait until the weekend, when Carobee would come fly them to Mt. Ice Cream. "This is going to be a trip to remember," she said, grinning.

CHAPTER

3

Up, Up, and Away

Dash sat on the edge of the Gummy Forest dock, swinging her feet in the Vanilla Sea. She reached down and splashed her arms with the cool water. She sighed. Dash did not like waiting!

Squinting, Dash checked the sky. Not only was she waiting for her friends, she was also expecting Carobee. The green-and-purple dragon would be hard to miss! At one time Dash and her friends were afraid of him. Now they considered him a true friend.

Finally Melli and Cocoa arrived. They flew to the edge of the dock and sat down next to Dash.

"How are you feeling?" Melli asked. She peered closely at her minty friend. "Are you okay, Dash?"

"I'm fine, really," Dash said.

Cocoa looked more closely at her. "Are you sure? You don't look so well."

"And your voice is a little hoarse," Melli added.

Dash stood up. She coughed to clear her throat. "I'm fine. Today we're going to Mt. Ice Cream." She pointed out to the horizon. "*Nothing* is going to stop me from feeling good or going on this trip."

Raina laughed as she walked up the dock.

"I'd say that today is double-dip delicious," she said. "I am so excited to spend some time on Meringue Island." She pulled a notebook from her bag. "I've made a list of all the historical places that I would love to explore." Reaching into her bag again, she pulled out a thick book. "I've been reading up on the island, and there are so many cool sights."

"I know," Melli agreed. She moved closer to Raina. "Can I see that book? I was hoping to learn more about the Meringue Cliffs and the fairies who live there."

"Let's not forget that there's an ice cream festival," Cocoa said with a grin. "There will be lots of chocolate ice cream for me!"

"There are so many sites to see. I can't wait!" Melli said.

 133

"Not to mention seeing Fruli's house," Cocoa added. "Berry thinks it's going to be gorgeous."

"Who cares about all that?" Dash said. She kept her eyes on the horizon. In the pale morning light she could barely make out the outline of Mt. Ice Cream. "Double Dip is one of the most challenging courses." She pointed to a crate at the end of the dock. "And I built an extraordinary sled. We're going to win!"

Cocoa held up her hand and Dash slapped a high five. "You can say that again, partner!" Cocoa said.

Dash stood up. "All I can think about is Double Dip," she said. "I can't wait to take first prize." She reached over and grabbed Cocoa's hand, raising it up in the air for a winning pose. "How do we look?" she asked.

"So mint!" Berry said as she flew in. "Is this the winning team of Double Dip?"

"Sure as sugar!" Dash and Cocoa said at the same time.

Raina started to laugh. "Berry, you know this is just a two-day trip, right?" She pointed to the large bags that Berry was holding in her hands.

"Those are two of the largest suitcases I've ever seen!" Melli gasped.

Berry laughed. "These cases are empty," she said, smiling. "I had to bring bags for all the clothes that I'm going to buy on Meringue Island!"

Dash rolled her eyes. "Of course," she said. "You are going to go to all of Fruli's favorite stores, right?"

Raising her eyebrows, Berry sighed. "I'm not sure I can afford all the stores where Fruli shops," she said. "Meringue Island has some of the fanciest stores in Sugar Valley. But I'm hoping to find some sweet deals."

"Or get some ideas for your own clothes," Melli said. "I think you're the best designer, Berry."

Berry blushed. "Thanks, Melli," she said. "I plan on buying lots of fabric."

"I hope that Carobee gets here soon," Dash said. She flew up in the air with her hand shielding her eyes, and then she started coughing nonstop.

"Dash, you sound awful!" Cocoa said.

Dash grabbed her throat. Her voice had sounded like a baby caramella bird's hoarse chirp.

"Oh, Dash," Raina said. "Your voice!"

Reaching into her backpack, Dash pulled out her thermos. She took a few sips of the liquid and cleared her throat. "There," she said, her voice sounding a little clearer. "Told you it was nothing that some soothing warm mint tea couldn't fix."

Her friends looked at her, unsure if Dash was really all right.

"Where is Carobee?" Dash continued. "I can't wait to get out on the slopes and take this sled for a spin. Right, Cocoa?"

Cocoa nodded, but she looked concerned. "Maybe you should just rest when we get to Fruli's," she said.

"Rest?" Dash snapped. "No way. There's too much to do today!" Then she pointed up to the sky. "And look, here comes Carobee!" Dash's heart began to race. Off in the distance she could see the immense span of Carobee's wings. Seeing her dragon friend made the journey to Double Dip very real! She waved her arms wildly and jumped up and down. "Over here, Carobee!" she cried. "We're ready for a winning adventure!"

CHAPTER 4

Sailing over the Sea

Carobee sailed down to the dock with his wide lavender wings. He gracefully bowed his head. "Hello," he greeted the fairies. "I am so happy to see all of you."

"And we are happy to see you," Dash said. She coughed a little, and then her face turned bright red. She couldn't stop coughing!

"Dash," Carobee said, "what's the matter? Are you okay?"

"Have some nectar," Raina said, holding out her bottle.

"That cough is getting worse," Melli muttered.

Dash fluttered her wings and flew over to her bag. Again she took out her thermos and gulped some warm mint tea. "I'll be fine," she finally managed to say. "It's not that bitter! I have my mint tea and mint drops."

"I know you always say that there's nothing mint can't cure," Melli said, "but your cough sounds terrible."

Raina stepped closer to her. "Maybe this trip isn't the best idea."

"I'm all right," Dash said firmly. "Please stop looking at me with those worried eyes!"

 140

She wished her friends would stop staring at
her! Yes, her cough was a sour drip on the day,
but she wasn't going to let that spoil everything.
She just had to race in Double Dip! She wasn't

about to decline a great racing invitation—not for anything!

"Is everyone ready?" Dash asked in a much clearer voice. She took a deep breath, grateful that the tea had soothed her cough and that her voice sounded almost normal.

Berry took out long licorice ropes from one of her suitcases. "I thought that these would come in handy."

Dash was thankful that Berry had changed the subject. She grabbed one of the ropes and carefully draped the licorice around Carobee's neck.

"This is perfect," Dash told Berry. "Thank you for remembering to bring this licorice! It wouldn't be safe without a rope to hold on to as we flew."

"Remember how Mogu gave us those black

licorice ropes at Candy Castle for our journey across the Vanilla Sea?" Melli asked.

"Never would I have imagined that we'd use those ropes for flying on a dragon," Dash said, smiling at Carobee.

"I think that was the kindest thing Mogu has ever done for anyone," Cocoa said.

"Just proves how scared he was of the *gooey goblins*!" Melli said, giggling.

Dash glanced up at the sky. "Come on, everyone. We should get going," she said. "I want to get to Cone Harbor."

"Yes!" Cocoa cheered. "I can't wait to see the mounds of ice cream at the festival."

"And all those delicious toppings," Raina said, licking her lips. "I read in the *Daily Scoop* that this year there are even more candy toppings for the ice cream, grand parties, and even more rides than ever before. The crowds are supposed to be huge."

Melli took a newspaper from her backpack. "I have that article here!" she said. She unfolded the paper and then held it up to show her friends. "This festival is going to be the best ever."

Dash held up her hand. "Are we all forgetting about Double Dip? That is the real highlight," she said, grinning.

"Sure as sugar," Cocoa said, giving her friend a tight squeeze. "If we get in early enough, we should take a practice run."

Cocoa's idea made Dash smile. She knew that she had picked the right partner! Clearly, Cocoa understood the value of practice!

The friends climbed onto the dragon's back. They sat in a row, with Dash in the lead spot.

"How is Nillie?" Raina asked.

Nillie was the secret sea horse who ruled the Vanilla Sea. Dash scanned the sea below, looking for her. The fairies had once been frightened of Nillie, but the sea horse had proved to be a great friend and a huge help to them—just like Carobee.

"Would you like to say hello?" Carobee asked.

Before Dash could yank on the licorice rope to stop him, Carobee swooped down close to the sea. All Dash wanted to do was get out to the slopes of Double Dip. She wasn't interested in any detours!

The other fairies cheered loudly as they looked for the gentle sea horse. Two horselike heads surfaced near the water.

"Over there!" Cocoa called, pointing.

Carobee shifted to the left and got closer to

the sea. "Hello, Sprinkle and Bean!" the dragon roared.

Nillie's twins, who guarded the sea, surfaced. They were surprised to see the Candy Fairies on the dragon's back.

"Everything all right?" Bean asked.

"Yes!" Dash replied. "We're off to the Cone Harbor Festival. Cocoa and I are racing in Double Dip."

Sprinkle jumped up and did a double flip. "Good luck," he cheered.

"Stop by on your trip home," Bean called as Carobee lifted higher up, away from the water.

"We'll come show you our medals!" Cocoa said. She smiled at Dash. "Our first-place medals!"

Dash was happy that Cocoa was excited. She admired her spirit and her positive outlook. She flashed Cocoa a smile. "We'll be the sweetest team ever," she said.

"Choc-o-rific!" Cocoa cheered.

"Wow," Dash said, peering over Carobee's wing. The view from the dragon's back was spectacular. Being up so high, the fairies could see all of Sugar Valley and the clear waters of the Vanilla Sea. They all settled down for a smooth ride high in the clouds. The sea seemed to stretch out forever. Soon Dash spotted Rock Candy Isle and knew that it wouldn't be too long until they saw the peaks of Meringue Island.

"Look over there," Melli said, pointing down below. "I see Cone Harbor!"

Carobee was heading straight for the shores of Meringue Island. Even from far away, they could see there were heaps of ice cream in large buckets and a wide assortment of candy on display.

"Licking lollipops," Berry gasped. "Look at all the Candy Fairies who are here."

Dash surveyed the scene below. Berry was right. Candy Fairies from all over Sugar Valley crowded the beach to take part in the beginning of the festival. Dash's wings tingled as she watched from Carobee's back. And then her nose began to itch. She didn't want to sneeze again and worry her friends, so she tried to stifle her sneeze. Luckily, her friends were so drawn into the scene in the harbor that no one noticed.

"Look at those carnival rides!" Melli shouted.

"And all that ice cream," Cocoa said, her eyes wide.

"I wish this festival was longer than just a weekend," Raina added.

Carobee touched down on the sugar sand. "Here you are," he said. "Welcome to Meringue Island!"

"The sweetest words ever!" Berry exclaimed. "And look, there's Fruli!" She spotted her glamorous friend in the crowd and jumped off Carobee's back.

"I've never seen Berry move so fast," Raina joked.

"She has a plan," Dash said. "Just like me." She winked at Cocoa. "Only I don't plan to be flying around stores. I'll be flying down the Double Dip course!"

Melli nudged Cocoa's arm and nodded.

"What?" Dash asked.

"We think that maybe it would be a good idea for you to go back to Fruli's house to rest,"

Cocoa said. "It was a long ride from Gummy Forest, so we should just take it easy."

"Rest?" Dash asked. "Are you kidding? We've got to get in a practice run!" As she started to get excited her voice gave out, and she started coughing once again.

Cocoa put her arm around Dash. "We'll run the course in the morning. It's been a long day." She handed Dash her thermos of hot peppermint tea.

Dash took some tea and then followed her friends over to see Fruli.

Maybe a good night's sleep would help my cough, she thought.

Though she wasn't sure how she was going to sleep! Being so close to Mt. Ice Cream was making her anything but tired!

CHAPTER 5

Sweet Home

W elcome to Meringue Island!" Fruli cried, greeting her friends. "How was your trip here?"

"A smooth ride," Dash said, grinning. "Thanks to Carobee."

Fruli waved at the green-and-purple dragon over by the shore. Then she turned to her friends. "Come on," she said. "There are going to be lots of celebrations tonight. This year's festival is going to be the biggest yet!"

"Are there many racers for Double Dip?" Dash asked.

Berry laughed. "Dash has a one-track mind," she said to Fruli.

"And it's the fast track!" Cocoa added. "Dash and I are going to race together."

Fruli nodded. "Yes, Berry told me. You will have some tough competition," she said. "Menta and Peppa are racing again this year. They have won the past two years in a row."

"Yes, we know," Dash said, looking around at all the fairies in the harbor.

"Menta is a little pushy," Fruli said. "And her sister, Peppa, is not much nicer. They have a reputation for fighting all the time, but they *are* fantastic racers."

Dash didn't want to admit it, but she was a little worried. The sisters would be hard to beat since they knew the course so well. It was very challenging—lots of double dips, and that slick chocolate slope. But Dash would have a Chocolate Fairy with her. She hoped that key ingredient in her plan would help win the race.

"I know about the mint sisters," Dash told Fruli. "But Cocoa and I are . . ." Her hoarse voice trailed off into a deep, barking cough.

"We are going to win," Cocoa finished for her. She handed Dash her thermos. "Here, Dash, drink some more. And maybe try not talking."

"That's not going to be easy for Dash," Melli

said. "But I bet resting your voice will help."

Fruli shook her head. "Oh, Dash," she said. "I'm so sorry you are sick."

"I'm not sick," Dash replied. Only this time, hardly any sound came out of her mouth when she spoke. Her blue eyes widened.

Why is this happening? she thought. *Why now?*

Cocoa took the thermos from Dash. "Don't worry," she said. "You'll get some rest tonight. We have another day before the race."

Dash wasn't sure what to think. She felt so tired, but she wanted—and needed—to practice. Her head was beginning to spin, so she followed her friend towards Fruli's house. As they flew over Cone Harbor they saw fairies setting up decorations for the start of the festival. There were colorful banners all along the harbor. Not

 156

everyone was all about the Double Dip race. There were many fairies in the harbor for the ice cream and the festive parties.

Up ahead, Dash saw meringue peaks and beautiful cloth canopies swaying in the breeze. Fruli's home looked like a castle!

All the fairies landed on the large terrace on the second floor and went inside. Berry turned around in a circle.

"Sweet strawberries!" Berry exclaimed. "This house is gorgeous!"

Fruli blushed. "This house has been in my family for a long time," she explained. "My great-grandparents built this place many years ago."

"They did a *sweet-tacular* job," Raina said, looking around. "There are so many details, and this fabric is delicious!" She touched one of the many lounge chairs.

"Everything is grown or made here on Meringue Island," Fruli said. "Please make yourselves comfortable. There are beds set up here in this room. I thought you would all like to stay together."

"Thank you," Berry said, speaking for her friends. "This is just perfect."

"Tonight we're hosting the Dip Party at our house. You are all invited to come," Fruli said. "I am going to change and then go downstairs to help."

Berry lugged her suitcase into the room. "Oh, I have a special outfit for tonight!" she exclaimed. "I sewed rainbow sprinkles onto my dress." She pulled the colorful dress out of her suitcase.

Dash stepped into the large bedroom. There were five beds with canopies draped over each one and thick comforters made of the softest cotton candy. Dash couldn't help but want to snuggle into a bed.

"Maybe I'll take a little rest before dinner," Dash said.

"That sounds like a good idea," Cocoa agreed. She put Dash's thermos next to her bed. "We'll wake you when we head downstairs."

Dash put her head down on the smooth pillow and in an instant was fast asleep. Thoughts of sledding filled her head, and she slept peacefully.

CHAPTER 6

A Minty Mess

Dash rolled over and opened one eye. For a second she didn't know where she was, and she quickly sat up. Cocoa was standing near her bed, peering down at her.

"Everyone!" Cocoa called over her shoulder. "She's up!" She sat down on the edge of the bed and looked over at Dash. "How do you feel?"

161

Rubbing her eyes, Dash leaned back on the soft pillows. She pulled the blanket up to her chin. And then she started to cough.

"That is a salty cough," Raina said, coming over to the bed. She handed Dash a large mug. "I just made you a fresh pot of peppermint tea. I hope this helps your throat."

Dash was grateful for the warm liquid and drank the whole mug before trying to speak. She looked behind Raina and Cocoa at the window on the far side of the room. Sunlight was streaming in and casting a bright light.

How can that be? Dash thought. *We got here before Sun Dip. What time is it?*

"You fell asleep last night," Cocoa told her. "We thought we'd let you sleep so you would feel better."

"You fell asleep in a second," Raina told her.

"And you didn't move all night," Melli added.

"Dash, you missed the Dip Party downstairs," Berry said, coming closer to the bed. "It was truly *sugar-tacular*! There were the most amazing candies, and the ice cream was delicious. And you should have seen Fruli's new dress. It was made of—"

Melli tugged at Berry's arm. Dash could tell that she was trying to get Berry to cool down on the descriptions of everything she'd missed last night. Berry was all juiced up about the grand party. The truth was, Dash didn't really care. She only wanted to head out to the slopes and try out her new double-dip sled.

"Sorry, Dash," Berry said softly. "I really missed you."

163

Dash smiled. "It's okay. I'm glad that you had fun."

"So, how do you feel now?" Cocoa asked. "I already waxed the sled with frosting. I know that you wanted to try to take a practice run this morning."

Melli gave Cocoa a hard look. "Do you think that is a good idea?" she asked.

Throwing off the covers, Dash leaped out of bed. "Sounds like a pure mint plan," she said.

"That peppermint tea did the trick, right?" Raina asked with a sly grin.

"You bet your peppermint leaves," Dash said.

Shaking her head, Melli looked concerned. "I'm not so sure about this," she said. "Dash, maybe you should stay in today, or at least this morning."

"The race is tomorrow," Dash said. She reached for her boots and slipped them on. "Cocoa and I have to try out the sled today. If there are any adjustments we need, we can make them tonight."

Berry handed Dash a small bag. "Take some

of these fruit chews," she told her. "I know the peppermint tea is helping your throat, but these chews should help you too."

"I need all the help I can get," Dash said. "Thanks, Berry." She turned to Cocoa. "Are you ready?"

"Sure as sugar!" Cocoa exclaimed. "We'll meet you in Cone Harbor for lunch," she said to her friends. "Berry, remember, you only have two suitcases!"

"Very funny," Berry said. "I plan to do lots of shopping, don't you worry!"

"And we're going to do some sightseeing," Raina said, smiling at Melli.

Dash laughed. "Sounds like we all have a plan for the day."

✦✦✦

Dash and Cocoa flew to Mt. Ice Cream and were surprised to find many fairy racers. The slopes were filled with fairies on double sleds trying out the icy slopes.

At the top of the mountain there was a large sign with a map of the trails. Double Dip was a five-sugar-cube-level course. This was the highest level in Sugar Valley. Dash noticed that Cocoa looked a little nervous.

"I know you haven't raced a course like this one," she said. "But don't worry, I'll help you out."

Cocoa pointed to the map. "I'm not sure about this part over here," she said. "I didn't realize that it's a *solid* chocolate area." She tilted her head as she thought through the problem. "Maybe we should try something different in that spot."

"What?" Dash said, not really listening. Her attention was focused on the starting line. Menta and Peppa were getting into their sleek new sugarcoated sled.

"Dash, are you listening to me?" Cocoa asked.

Turning her attention back to Cocoa, Dash pulled her goggles on. "Let's go check out the slope."

"But we need to have a race plan," Cocoa said. "If we know the slippery chocolate is coming up, we'll need to change our speed."

But Dash didn't hear a word—she was already flying toward the lineup. Cocoa shrugged and followed her.

At the starting line Dash jumped into the front of her sled. "Cocoa, since you're taller, you need to sit in the rear. You take the back."

Cocoa slipped into the sled and settled into her seat. She pulled her goggles over her eyes.

Dash couldn't help overhearing Peppa and Menta next to them. The sisters were screaming at each other!

"How green can you be?" barked Menta. She was glaring at her sister as Dash and Cocoa readied their sled for the run. "There is no way you can steer through that course without *me* telling *you* what to do."

Dash watched Peppa's face get redder and her eyes narrow at her sister. Peppa twisted her long hair up into a bun and then took a deep breath. "You are one to talk," she barked. "You almost took off the back blade on that last run. You need to listen to *me* out on the slope. I know what I'm doing."

"And I know what I am doing!" Menta argued back.

Dash glanced over at Cocoa. The rumors about the fighting sisters were true. And Dash could see why. The fairies were different in every way imaginable. Peppa had blond hair and was tall and thin. Menta had dark hair and was much shorter and wider. Dash wondered how they managed to win so many races with all their bickering.

"So these are the champions?" Cocoa whispered.

"Yes," Dash said. She watched as they took off down the slope. They sailed around the first turn, and then they were gone. "They always manage to win."

"Well, not this year!" Cocoa said, trying to sound enthusiastic.

 171

The two friends began their practice run. They sled through the first part of the course. Dash was yelling instructions to Cocoa and kept a close watch on their time. Feeling pleased with their run, Dash smiled to herself.

This is going to be a smooth race, she thought.

On the approaching turn to the chocolate slope, the sled began to slip. Dash held on tight.

"It's the chocolate!" Cocoa shouted over the rushing wind. "We need to slow down as we make the turn!"

"But we'll lose time," Dash said anxiously. She leaned back to speak to Cocoa. She couldn't turn around. She had to keep her eyes on the course. "We can't slow down!" she shouted. "I know what I'm doing!"

"Cold chocolate gets very slick," Cocoa

advised. "This part of the slope is dangerous."

Dash tried to respond, but no sound came out of her mouth. Her yelling made her throat tickle, and then the coughing started again. As she coughed she lost control of the sled. The sled rammed into a scoop of chocolate fudge swirl.

Cocoa jumped out of the sled. "What are you doing?" she barked. "You can't just turn off the course like that!" Then Cocoa realized Dash had crashed because of her coughing.

Quickly Cocoa gave her friend the thermos. Only this time, the tea didn't soothe the cough. Dash's whole face was red, and her eyes were filled with tears.

Dash felt woozy. There was no denying the fact that she was sick. And now the sled was damaged. This was a giant minty mess.

CHAPTER

7

Double Mint Mistake

Dash was still coughing and showing no sign of stopping.

In her pocket Dash found the fruit chews that Berry had given her. She started to suck on the treats, and her throat began to feel better. At least she could stop coughing! She flew out of the sled and checked the damage to the front blades.

Dash looked down at the ground. First no voice and now no sled. Things were looking pretty bitter.

"What's going on?" Raina called out. She flew up to her friends with Berry and Melli close behind. "We were just coming to see how you were doing."

Melli examined the damaged sled. "Are you all right?" she asked. "Looks like a bad crash."

Cocoa stood up and flapped her wings. "We're fine," she said. "I'm not so sure about the sled, though." She knelt down and looked at the bent front blades. "But we need to get Dash back to Fruli's house. She doesn't have a voice at all now. And she nearly got us buried in ice cream because she couldn't stop barking orders—or coughing!"

Dash wanted to answer, but she found she still couldn't speak at all. She stuck her lip out.

Of all the minty things to go wrong, she thought. *This is a bitter disaster!*

"Let's get you both back to Fruli's," Berry said. "Raina and I will take the sled. I'm sure we can fix it up."

Dash's head was swirling too fast to argue about anything else. The thought of lying in that cozy, soft bed at Fruli's house was so appealing to her. She wanted to close her eyes and forget about her fight with Cocoa, the crash, and the damaged sled.

Back at Fruli's house, Dash climbed into bed. Melli puffed up the pillows so that she wouldn't cough so much when she put her head down.

Fruli took Dash's temperature and shook her head. "It's official," she said. "Dash is sick."

Dash was miserable. All she could do was close her eyes. Before she drifted off to sleep, she overheard Cocoa and Melli talking.

"She was supersalty," Cocoa told Melli. "Maybe I was being a little too strong-willed on the chocolate slope, but Dash wasn't listening to me at all."

"What do you mean?" Melli asked. "You are a Chocolate Fairy! If anyone knows chocolate, it's you!"

"Dash is the experienced rider," Cocoa said. "Only she was so minty! She kept yelling at me the whole time."

"Sometimes Dash is a little too fast for her own good," Raina added.

Dash was *still* bitter. How could Cocoa say that about her? She turned over and faced the wall. And since she couldn't tell anyone how she felt, she fell into a deep sleep.

When Dash woke up, she was surprised to find Berry sitting by her side, sewing a beautiful pink-and-orange fabric. Dash guessed that it was a new purchase from the morning's shopping spree.

"Hi, Dash," Berry said brightly. "Have some ice cream shake. It is so delicious." She handed her a tall glass with a pink straw. "I'm sure the cold ice cream will feel good on your sore throat."

Berry was right, and Dash enjoyed the soothing cold drink. She sat up and looked around the empty room. She was sure that Berry would rather be out shopping.

She tried to talk, but still no words came out. Berry reached for a pad of paper and a pen and handed them to Dash. "Kinda like sending a sugar fly message without the fly!" Berry joked.

Dash quickly wrote out her message and handed the pad to Berry.

Berry laughed. "Oh, Dash," she said. "I can always go shopping! But I came to see you race Double Dip, and you are going to get better for the race."

Dash stared out the window at Mt. Ice Cream. The view from the window was extraordinary, and she could even see the Double Dip course. There were some sleds on the mountain, and Dash felt a lump in her stomach. Without

practice time, she and Cocoa would be at a huge
disadvantage. She hung her head.

Who am I kidding? Dash thought. *Cocoa is so
angry at me. She probably doesn't even want to race
with me anymore.*

"Cheer up," Berry said.

Dash took the pad of paper and wrote another
note. She handed the paper to Berry.

"Yes," she said. "Cocoa is with Raina and Fruli."

Dash walked out to the balcony and sank down onto one of the lounge chairs. Cone Harbor Festival happened once a year. Of all the times for her to feel sick—and to be fighting with her friend! This was a doubly minty mistake.

Berry came and sat down at the foot of her bed. "Don't feel so sad," she said. "Fruli and the others will be back."

All Dash knew was that being sick and angry was not a good combination. She closed her eyes and hoped that she would be feeling better soon.

CHAPTER 8

A Sweeter Way

Dash spent the afternoon sitting on the balcony at Fruli's house. She still wasn't able to speak, and her throat felt very sore. Being sick and away from home was not fun, but at least here she could still look out and see Mt. Ice Cream. Dash couldn't take her eyes off the action on the slopes. There were many sleds racing down the mountain. She wished that she could be taking practice runs too.

If only I had a racing partner and *a sled,* she thought sadly.

Dash sank down lower in the chair.

"Do you want anything?" Berry asked. All afternoon Berry had kept asking her if she wanted anything. Berry's being sweet to her wasn't helping Dash's mood at all.

"You have to try these meringue cookies," Berry said. She held out a plate to Dash. When Dash refused, Berry shook her head. "It's not like you to turn down a snack."

Dash didn't feel like eating. In fact, she didn't feel like doing anything.

"Hi, Dash!" Melli called from above. She flew down and landed next to Dash's lounge

chair. "Guess what? I was able to find some extra-gooey caramel to fix your sled. It will be as good as new now." She held out a pail of golden syrup.

Dash reached over for her pad of paper. She quickly wrote a note to Melli and handed it to her.

"You're welcome," Melli said after she read the note. "And yes, I do think that you'll be able to race tomorrow." Then she turned to Berry. "Have Fruli, Raina, and Cocoa come back yet?"

"No," Berry said. "Not yet."

Melli smiled at Dash. "Do you feel better?"

Wishing that she did feel better, Dash shook her head. This day was not turning out how she had planned.

Berry pointed up to the sky. "Look, here they come!" she said.

Dash sat up and saw Fruli leading Raina and Cocoa to the balcony. Fruli was holding a small rectangular box. She imagined that her friends had all had a great time—even without her.

"Hi, Dash!" Raina said. "I'm glad to see you sitting out here."

With a little shrug, Dash nodded. She didn't take her eyes off the small white box in Fruli's hands.

"Mission complete?" Berry asked.

"Sure as sugar," Cocoa gloated.

Dash wondered what her friends were talking about.

Raina sat down on a chair next to Dash. "After you fell asleep last night, I was reading through the Fairy Code Book," Raina told her. "I read a story about a Candy Fairy who had a

 187

bad sore throat. As I was reading to everyone
Fruli remembered the story too."

"She remembered about the ice cream sandwiches!" Cocoa blurted out. "And I made the
chocolate cookie part of the treat."

Dash faced Cocoa. She couldn't believe
Cocoa was talking to her and that she had gone
to all the trouble of making her a healing treat.
Her friends hadn't been just out celebrating at
the festival.

"I felt bad about our fight, Dash," Cocoa said,
moving closer to her. "I was stubborn too. And
then with you getting sick, I knew that I had to
do something. I hope this works."

Fruli stepped forward. "The ice cream from
the far side of the mountain is known to have
healing powers," she said. "With Cocoa's help,

we made these mini mint-chip ice cream sandwiches."

"Go ahead," Cocoa said. "Try one."

Fruli opened the box. In three neat rows were
twelve mini round sandwiches. Dash didn't
know what to say. She picked one up and took
a bite. The rich chocolate outside went so nicely
with the minty ice cream. Dash closed her eyes
as the cold ice cream slid down her sore throat.

"So mint," Dash said. Her eyes grew wider.
Her voice was back!

"Well, that was fast!" Melli said, grinning.

"Do you feel different?" Raina asked, leaning forward.

Dash reached for another mini ice cream sandwich. "I'll have another one to be sure," she said brightly.

"The mint ice cream remedy has helped fairies on the island for centuries," Fruli explained.

Pulling out the Fairy Code Book, Raina flipped to the chapter about the healing ice cream. "See?" she said. "Here is the story about those healing ice cream sandwiches. I'm so glad that I stumbled upon the story last night. And that Fruli knew just where to find the ice cream!"

"Thank you," Dash said. "Thank you to all of you for being so sweet to me. I know that I've been a bit minty."

"We understand," Berry said. "No one likes being sick."

"Especially the day before a big race," Melli added.

Dash groaned. "I can't believe the race is tomorrow."

Raina pulled a map from her bag. "Maybe this will help?" she said. "I got this from a booth near the starting line. It's the whole course. I know it's not the same as actually racing, but you and Cocoa can study the route and come up with a good strategy for the race. This map shows all the trails and toppings along the way."

"And with the caramel that Melli got today, I can fix the sled," Cocoa told Dash. She squeezed Dash's hand. "Please say that you'll do this. I want to make this happen. I really want to win."

 191

"Sure as sugar," Dash said. She sat up and studied the map.

"Teamwork is always the fastest way to the finish line," Melli said.

"And Peppa and Menta don't have that going for them at all!" Cocoa exclaimed. "You should have heard them today in town."

"It was hard for anyone not to hear them," Fruli said. "They were screaming at each other from one store or booth to another!"

"Those two will never cross the finish line," Berry said, shaking her head.

Dash had to agree. And she was grateful for Raina's clever thinking. If they couldn't be on the slopes, the next best thing was to at least *study* the slopes!

Together, Dash and Cocoa talked over the

course using a sugar hair clasp from Berry's collection as the sled. Melli wrote down what they said so that they could have a record to help them remember the plan for the race.

"We might have a chance," Dash said.

"We have a double-good chance!" Cocoa said with a smile. "I'm glad we're not fighting anymore."

"Me too," Dash said, grinning. "It's much sweeter this way!"

9

Green as Mint

That night, instead of heading down to the harbor, the fairies stayed at Fruli's house. They all thought Dash needed one more night of rest, and no one wanted to leave her.

"We can watch the fireworks from the balcony," Fruli said. "When I was a little fairy, I used to watch from this spot. We have a good view of Cone Harbor. We can have a picnic out here and avoid all the crowds."

"Sounds delicious to me," Berry said happily.

"I can't wait," Melli added.

Dash was glad that her friends wanted to be with her. And she was very happy to be feeling healthier.

True to Fruli's word, the view was perfect. The fairies felt as if they had front-row seats for the colorful fireworks.

"The fireworks are *sugar-tastic*!" Melli said, enjoying the special seats.

"We appreciate you having us all," Raina told her.

"I'm happy you could all be here," Fruli replied. "And I'm very glad that Dash is feeling better. I can't wait for the race tomorrow."

 195

"Me neither!" Dash and Cocoa said at the same time.

Right before the lights were turned out for the night, Dash gathered her friends together on her bed. "Your trip to Meringue Island isn't what you had planned," she said sadly. "Berry, your shopping time was cut short. And Raina and Melli, you didn't get lots of sightseeing done."

"I did eat lots of chocolate ice cream," Cocoa said, rubbing her belly.

Dash hung her head. "Berry, it wasn't fair you had to stay in all day with me, and the rest of you worked so hard on those ice cream sandwiches and fixing the sled."

"Fair?" Berry asked, raising her dark eyebrows up high. "Fair, fair, lemon square. You would have done the same for each of us. I'm just so

 196

happy to hear your voice again!" She walked over to her bed and pulled out a bag that she had put underneath the cotton-candy blanket. "And now for my surprise!" she declared. She held up two sparkling pink and orange sledding outfits. "I made you and Cocoa matching racing suits!"

Dash laughed. "Berry, those are *so mint*!"

Berry grinned. "I was hoping you'd say that!"

"Now get some rest so you'll be perfect for the race," Cocoa ordered. She gave her friend a tight squeeze. "Sweet dreams."

Curling up in her pink bed, Dash fell off to sleep. She had the best friends in the whole world. She couldn't wait for the sun to rise and for the race day to begin. With her friends beside her, she was ready for whatever happened.

The next morning, Dash's fever was gone. When she opened her eyes, she felt minty fresh. She sprang out of bed and went out to the balcony, where she found Cocoa already dressed and ready for the day. She was carefully inspecting the sled.

"Good morning," Cocoa said when she saw Dash. "How are you feeling?"

"Fresh as a new mint leaf," Dash boasted. "Those ice cream sandwiches were the perfect healing treat."

Cocoa smiled. "I knew that you'd be fine for today. The sled looks perfect, don't you think?"

Dash leaned down and checked the sled. She had to admit that Cocoa and Melli had done a fine job of mending the front blades.

"Sweet sugar," Dash said, "this is a winner!"

"I added this chocolate bar in the back to steady the sled a little bit," Cocoa said. She pointed to the addition on the end. "What do you think?"

Dash surveyed the change. "I'd say that having a Chocolate Fairy as a teammate was the smartest choice I could have made," she replied. "I never would have thought of that and I know that it will help over the slick chocolate part of the course."

Cocoa stood up with her chest puffed out proudly. "Aw, sweet chips," she said. "Thanks. I hope this all works out."

"Are mint leaves green?" Dash exclaimed. "This sled is made for first place." She stood tall.

"And this win will be even sweeter because we'll win the race together."

The two fairies hugged. Dash knew that fighting with a friend was salty business but making up was the sweetest part.

"Come on," she said to her sledmate. "Let's get going."

The two fairies quickly ate their breakfast and headed to the top of Mt. Ice Cream. There were many fairy teams lined up ready to race, and the grandstands were full of cheering fairies. Cocoa looked nervous.

"Don't worry," Dash said. "We're going to follow our plan." She looked Cocoa in the eye. "I trust you. And you trust me."

Cocoa smiled. "One hundred and fifty chocolate percent!" she said, grinning.

To the left of them, Peppa and Menta were pulling up their sled. Dash noticed that theirs was the newest model in the Sweet Slider 5000 series—the most expensive sled on the market. But she held her head high. She knew that her sled had been made with careful thought.

"Don't pull that," Peppa barked at her sister. She flipped her blond hair over to one side.

"It's fine," growled Menta.

Dash and Cocoa nodded to each other. Melli was right. If those two kept fighting, surely they would lose.

Even though the sisters were wearing matching outfits, they were definitely not racing the same race. They couldn't even agree on where to leave their sled while they signed in at the judges' table!

The giant clock clanged, and all riders were called to the official starting line.

Dash spotted their friends in the stands. It was hard to miss Berry in her new colorful outfit.

"I guess Berry did get to shop this morning," Dash whispered to Cocoa.

"She's dressed to win," Cocoa said. "So let the races begin!"

As all the sleds lined up, Dash felt the tension growing. Everyone there wanted to take home first prize. She looked back at Cocoa. "Are you ready?" she asked, pulling down her snow goggles.

"You bet your chocolate chips I am!" Cocoa said.

TWEEEEEET! The starting whistle blew!

"Then let's win this race!" Dash shouted.

CHAPTER
10

Double Sweet

As the cold air pushed against Dash's face, she smiled. She had dreamt of this moment for a long time. Being out on the slopes of Mt. Ice Cream felt incredible! Yesterday she didn't think that she'd be able to feel the speed of sledding down the slick, icy slopes.

"Holy peppermint!" Dash screamed. "Here we go!"

All around her were double sleds with determined fairies. She tried to stay focused and gripped her wheel tightly. There was nothing like the rush of a fast race downhill.

"First turn, coming up," Cocoa said from behind.

Even though the pair had not run the entire course, they both felt that they knew all the curves and dips of the mountain. By studying the map, they had prepared themselves well. Dash kept her legs straight heading into the curve, knowing that a sharp left was coming up.

"Sweet syrup!" Dash cried as their sled pulled ahead of five others. If all the Mint Fairies in

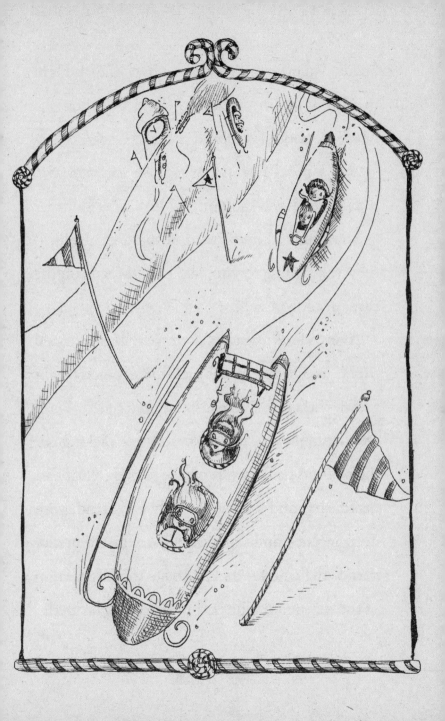

Sugar Valley could see her now! She thought of Minny and how excited she'd be when she heard all about Dash's adventure.

And maybe I'll be able to show her the shiny first-place medal, Dash thought.

She squinted and stared at the trail ahead. If they were going to win, she had to focus on the race, not the prize!

A few yards ahead of their sled, Dash spotted Menta and Peppa. It was hard to miss their bright green outfits and cotton-candy-pink sled. Dash wondered if they spent as much time picking out their outfits as they did on the slopes. Her heart beat faster, and she had to slow her breath with deep inhales and exhales. Now was the tricky part of the course—the chocolate topping section of the mountain. She had to stay clear headed!

"You all right?" Dash called back.

"Yes," Cocoa shouted over the wind. "Here comes the chocolate!"

As they closed in on Menta and Peppa, Dash could hear them fighting.

"Stay the course!" Dash called back as they headed toward the slick, hard chocolate.

"Slow down," Cocoa said. "We have to take this curve slowly."

Dash's instinct was to push forward, but she remembered what had happened during their practice run. This time she listened to her Chocolate Fairy friend. The extra chocolate weight in the back of the sled helped them steady the sled on the turn. Dash was grateful for Cocoa's clever chocolate planning. They rounded the bend and sailed past Peppa and Menta!

"Who was that?" Peppa snapped as Dash and Cocoa sped by.

Sure as sugar, their plan had worked!

The finish line was straight ahead. Dash couldn't believe they were so close. She wasn't sure if Peppa and Menta were behind or next to them. Dash squeezed the wheel and held tight as the sled soared ahead.

Down the mountain they sped. Dash felt the finish-line ribbon break as the sled crossed over the cherry-red stripe drizzled on the ice.

"Sweet chocolate chips!" Cocoa cheered. "Dash, we did it!"

In a flash their friends surrounded their sled. There was lots of hugging and cheering. Dash reached out to Cocoa.

"Winning has never been so sweet!" she said.

Princess Lolli, the gentle and kind ruler of Sugar Valley, flew over to the winners. "Congratulations," she said, beaming with pride. "You were *sugar-tastic* out there. Well done."

"Thank you," Dash and Cocoa said together.

"Come," Princess Lolli said. She was holding two shiny sugarcoated medals in her hand. "Fly with me over to the winner's circle. We need to present the two of you with your first-place prize."

Dash was overwhelmed by all the attention. There were so many fairies! She gripped Cocoa's hand. She was glad her friend was with her.

The *Daily Scoop* had a few reporters taking interviews and photographs.

"Congratulations," a reporter with orange wings called out. She was holding a notepad in her hand. "Please tell me your names."

"Dash and Cocoa," Dash proudly told her.

"How does it feel to win Double Dip?" she asked.

"Sweet as sugar!" Dash replied.

Dash spotted Menta and Peppa off to the side. They weren't arguing anymore. For the first time, they were speechless. Dash felt sorry for them. She knew that losing a race didn't feel good at all.

"We had some great competition out there," Dash went on to say. "It was a tough race. Everyone out there did a great job. And I'd like to thank my sledmate, Cocoa. She is a true friend and a dedicated racer."

The crowd cheered, and Cocoa gave Dash a tight squeeze.

"I owe so much to Dash," Cocoa said into the microphone. "She taught me everything!"

Princess Lolli slipped the medals over the winners' heads and posed with them for a picture for the paper. Then she turned to the crowd. "Who's ready for some treats?"

The crowd roared in response and moved toward the harbor.

"Oh, this is my favorite part of the festival," Fruli said as she reached Dash and Cocoa. "And the winner of the race gets to make the first double dip."

"What is a double dip?" Dash asked.

"It's an ice-cream cone that you dip in two toppings. You can't just have one, there are so many toppings at the festival!"

Dash checked out all the barrels lined up on

the stage. "Everything is always better with a touch of mint," she said with a grin. She dipped her cone in mint and then in mini chocolate chips. "To honor two great tastes and team-mates!"

Everyone laughed, and Cocoa held out her cone. "Hit me with some mint too," she said.

Dash happily dipped Cocoa's cone. Sure, friends argue, but the sweetest part of friendship is making up. This certainly was a double-dip celebration!

Jelly Bean Jumble

For Karen Nagel,

who makes my books extra sweet!

1

Sweet Surprise Lunch

The sun shone down on the Royal Gardens at Candy Castle. Berry the Fruit Fairy sat under a lollipop tree with her friend Raina, a Gummy Fairy. "It feels like everyone in Candy Kingdom is outside today," Berry said.

"On a day like this, it's hard to stay inside,"

Raina replied. She tilted her face up toward the sun's rays.

Berry smiled. It was the first warm day of spring, and all the fairies in Sugar Valley were buzzing around. After the chilly winter, the warm sunshine was a welcome feeling.

"Thanks for meeting me for lunch today," Berry told her. "I'm sorry I missed Sun Dip last night."

Sun Dip was a time when Candy Fairies gathered to talk about their day. During the last moments of daylight, Candy Fairies shared stories and sweet treats. Yesterday Berry had missed out on seeing her group of friends.

"Did you finish planting the jelly bean seedlings?" Raina asked.

Berry's wings fluttered. "Yes," she said. "I

needed the extra time last night. The seedlings are getting so tall. I planted them all."

"Princess Lolli is going to love the new crop of jelly beans," Raina said, smiling. "Our basket is going to be *sugar-tastic*!"

Berry and her friends were making a special basket for Princess Lolli's upcoming journey to see her sister, Princess Sprinkle. Princess Sprinkle lived on Cupcake Lake and ruled over Cake Kingdom to the north. Each sister brought the other the best of her kingdom's crops to share when she visited.

On her last visit, Princess Sprinkle had brought beautiful cupcakes, cakes, cookies, and brownies. The Cake Fairies were known for their tasty treats. The Candy Fairies always had a feast during those visits. For Princess Lolli's trip, Berry had wanted to give the fairies in Cake

Kingdom a special sweet treat of her own.

"Cocoa and Melli showed us the basket last night," Raina said. "They worked very hard and it is beautiful."

"And did Dash find the nighttime mints?" Berry asked. "I know she was worried about getting the right size mint for Princess Lolli to see near the Forest of Lost Flavors."

Raina shivered. "Oh, I don't like thinking of that place," she said. "All those white, flavorless trees . . ." Her voice trailed off.

Berry had heard many stories about the creepy forest from Raina. The Gummy Fairy loved books and owned the largest collection in Sugar Valley. There was plenty written about the Forest of Lost Flavors. The wide forest divided the land between Candy Kingdom and

Cake Kingdom. Most Candy Fairies stayed far away from the eerie forest. Nothing grew there anymore—no candy crops at all. Now there were just tall white trees without any flavor. That forest was not somewhere a fairy would want to be without any light, and it was scariest at night.

"I am sure Princess Lolli is going to love our basket," Berry said. "It is an honor to make her one for her trip. I don't remember the last time she went to see her sister."

"Princess Sprinkle has come here for the last few visits," Raina remarked. "Princess Lolli must be excited." She looked over at Candy Castle. "I wonder if she gets nervous about traveling such a far distance. I would!"

Berry reached for her fruit nectar drink. "I saw Butterscotch yesterday. She was looking forward to the flight. If I could ride Butterscotch there, I wouldn't be afraid."

Butterscotch was a royal unicorn. She was a beautiful caramel color with a deep-pink mane. She often took Princess Lolli on long voyages.

"Maybe," Raina said thoughtfully. "I'm not sure that's a trip I would want to make with Butterscotch, or any unicorn."

"I would take a unicorn ride any day!" Dash said, landing next to Berry.

"Dash!" Berry exclaimed. "Lickin' lollipops, you scared the sugar out of me."

Dash giggled. "Sorry," the small Mint Fairy said. "When Raina told me she was meeting you for lunch, I had to join in the fun."

"And so did we!" Melli said, flying in with Cocoa.

Berry looked at the Caramel and Chocolate Fairies in front of her. "You came to see me?"

"Sure as sugar!" Cocoa said. "We missed you last night."

"Were you talking about Princess Lolli's trip?" Melli asked. She sat down next to Berry. "I know Berry wishes she could go. Besides Meringue Island, Cake Kingdom is the leading place for fashion, right, Berry?"

Berry shrugged. "Well, Cake Kingdom does have some sweet styles," she said, thinking. "But I've never been there. I've only read about it in *Sugar Beat* magazine."

The five fairy friends settled down to eat their

lunch. It wasn't often that they got to see one another during the day. Usually, each of the fairies worked in a different part of the kingdom on her own candies. This was a sweet surprise lunch.

They had just finished eating when a burst of chilly air lifted Melli up off the ground. "Brrrr," she said, shivering. "What is going on? It was such a beautiful morning!"

"I think there's a storm coming," Cocoa said. She looked up to the sky and saw the dark clouds rushing overhead. "Bittersweet, I was so hoping for another warm night."

"That isn't going to happen," Dash said, slipping on her vest. She carefully wiggled her silver wings through the slots in the back. "Nothing like a brisk spring evening to get the mint flowing," she added. "And I have got some mighty mints

 226

to tend to. See you fairies later!" In a flash, Dash was gone. She wasn't known as the fastest fairy in Sugar Valley for nothing!

Melli wrapped her shawl tighter around her waist. "What about your seedlings, Berry?" she asked. "They are not going to like this blast of cold."

"Oh, it's not so bad," Berry told her. She looked up at the sky. "Winter has passed. Sure as sugar, the sun will warm us all tomorrow with another sunny day. I can't wait!"

Berry's friends shared a worried look. But they all agreed that by Sun Dip the next day they'd put their candies and finishing touches on the basket. They knew Princess Lolli was counting on them. And none of them wanted to disappoint the sweet fairy princess.

2

Sour Face

During the night a bitter storm traveled through Sugar Valley. The strong winds blew cold blasts, leaving a layer of frost all over the northern part of Candy Kingdom. Berry slept soundly through the night, not hearing the storm at all. Her work in Fruit Chew Meadow over the last few days had made her very tired.

When the Fruit Fairy woke up, she looked out her window. *What happened?* she thought. At first she thought she was still dreaming. She rubbed her eyes. But there, on the fruit slices outside her window, was frost! Thick frost. Cocoa had been right about a storm coming. And what a storm it had been!

"Oh no! The jelly bean plants!" Berry exclaimed. Her heart was racing as she looked out on the white, frosted gardens. She had to get to Fruit Chew Meadow! She wasn't sure what she would find when she arrived.

As Berry flew over the meadow, her heart was pounding. She had been so proud of those plants! She had tried new flavors and had carefully selected the seeds to create bold, bright oranges, reds, yellows, purples, and even pinks for this new crop. She had hoped these beans would be some of her finest work. But Berry's eyes widened when she saw her plants. Heavy ice weighed down the large leaves. Her once-tall seedlings were hunched over. The bright colors of her new spring candy were buried beneath the ice.

"Oh, sour sticks," Berry sighed. She leaned over

for a closer look. As she carefully brushed the ice off the leaves, her fingers tingled from the cold.

"Are you the fairy who planted those?" a voice behind her called.

Berry turned to see Razz, a know-it-all Fruit Fairy. She had the same name as Berry's grandmother, but was not nearly as sweet. Razz was standing right behind Berry with a mean look on her face. Her blond hair was in a high ponytail clasped with a lemon sparkle clip. "Those poor seedlings," Razz muttered. She crossed her arms tightly across her chest. "Planted by a Fruit Fairy who didn't know any better."

Razz had no business saying such bitter words. She was a little older than Berry and often tried to tell her what to do. She might have been a Fruit Fairy, but she always had on a sour-candy face.

"If these are your plants," Razz went on, "you should tend to them right away." She flapped her large orange wings. "A fairy with more experience would have known to wait until *after* the first spring frost to plant."

"The weather was perfect for planting," Berry burst out. She glared at Razz. Any other Fruit Fairy would have offered to help instead of pointing out the problem. Razz's bitter attitude was making everything worse.

Razz shook her head. "Aren't you friends with Raina? Isn't she that Gummy Fairy always quoting the Fairy Code Book?" Her blue eyes shot an icy stare, and Berry shivered. Then Razz chuckled. *"I read in the Fairy Code Book . . . ,"* she taunted, trying to sound like Raina.

Berry took a deep breath. It was true that

Raina always had the Fairy Code Book with her and was quick to quote from it. But there was such helpful information in the fairy history book. Berry didn't like the way Razz was talking about one of her best friends. Hot feelings were bubbling up inside of her, and she wanted to lash back.

"They'll be fine," Berry snapped. She glared back at Razz. She wasn't about to let Razz make her feel worse.

"Well, good luck with *that*," Razz said, tossing her ponytail. And then she flew off.

Alone in the meadow, Berry thought about what to do next. She was still bubbling inside. Razz just made her so red-cherry mad! Maybe she had jumped a little too quickly to plant the seedlings, but she had so desperately wanted

Princess Lolli to take a fresh, new crop with her to Cake Kingdom.

"Not this time," she said with a heavy sigh. Her jelly beans didn't look as if they stood a chance.

Berry sat down on the cold, frozen ground. This was not her first crop of jelly beans. She had planted plenty before. She should have known better. Berry gripped her hands into fists. "Oh," she muttered. "I should have said that to Razz! This is not my first crop of jelly beans!"

For a long time Berry sat looking at the plants. She wondered what would happen to the crop. She looked up at the blue sky. The storm had passed, but would there be another? Or would the sun come out and warm up the meadow? She knew that cold weather at this stage of

 235

growing jelly beans could change their flavor. There was nothing Berry liked less than a tasteless jelly bean. She slumped down and put her head in her hands.

Then Berry realized something. "Sweet strawberries!" she exclaimed. "Maybe Razz did say something helpful."

If there was any fairy who might know what to do, it was Raina. With that huge library of hers, maybe there'd be some information about how to tend to frozen seedlings. For a moment Berry's wings dipped down low to the ground. She didn't want to be entered in the Fairy Code Book as the Fruit Fairy who had ruined the first spring jelly bean crop.

But maybe there was still time to save them. In a flash, Berry headed to Gummy Forest.

3

Bitter Cold

Berry shivered as a cold gust pushed her wings back. She fought against the wind and headed down to Gummy Forest. Thinking back to yesterday, she remembered how proud and happy she had been. The warm sunshine had made the ground perfect for planting, and she had finished her work in the Fruit Chew

Meadow. Now her tasty, prize-winning jelly beans were freezing. If only she could turn back time and hold off on planting.

The wind made her wings feel heavy, but Berry traveled on. She had to get to Gummy Forest and talk to Raina.

As she arrived Berry noticed the land wasn't as frosted as in Fruit Chew Meadow. Maybe the tall trees in the forest protected the gummy plants. In Fruit Chew Meadow there were no trees, and the field was more open.

Raina fed the gummy fish at Gummy Lake every morning. Berry checked there first and felt a wave of relief when she saw Raina standing on the shoreline.

"Raina!" Berry called out. She flew over to her friend. "I am so happy you're here!"

Raina nearly dropped her basket of flavor flakes. When she saw Berry, she rushed over to her. "Berry, did you hear that storm last night?" she asked. "The winds were whipping around here. Many of the animals are still in hiding."

Berry shook her head. "I slept through the whole storm," she admitted. "This morning was a surprise. When I woke up, I saw there was an icy frost all over the meadow. And on the jelly bean seedlings!"

"Oh, sweet sugar," Raina replied, shaking her head. "I was afraid you were going to tell me that. This is more than a spring frost." She looked worried.

"I was hoping we could do some research," Berry said. "Maybe there is a story in the Fairy Code Book about a spring storm that could help us figure out how to save the frozen crops."

"Maybe," Raina said. "Tell me, how are the seedlings? How are the leaves?"

"They are very weak," Berry told her. Her fingers still tingled from brushing the ice off the jelly bean leaves. "I removed all the ice this morning. But I am afraid the damage has been done. If I don't help them now . . ." Berry stopped talking. She couldn't finish her sentence. She looked into Raina's kind eyes. She knew her friend understood how hard it was for her to talk about the damaged crops.

"Why don't you head back to my house," Raina said. She threw more of the flavor flakes in the lake. "While I finish up the gummy feedings, you can start doing some research."

"Thanks, Raina," Berry said, flying off. Raina had the best library in all of Candy Kingdom. If there was a book that could help her, she would find it in Raina's library. "I'll see you soon."

Inside Raina's house Berry was overwhelmed by the selection of books. She started pulling down books from the shelves. Flipping through the pages, she searched for anything about a spring frost. She flew from one end of the room to the other. Not one book she looked at helped her at all.

"What happened in here?" Raina exclaimed. She stood at the door with her mouth gaping open.

Berry looked up from the book in her hand. She saw the mess she had made of Raina's home. There were open books tossed around the room. Berry could tell from Raina's expression that she was not happy. Raina was all about order and kept her books neatly organized and lined up on her shelves.

"Sorry," Berry said softly. She gently closed the book she was holding and put it carefully back on a shelf.

Before Raina could say anything, a sugar fly appeared with a message. Raina took the note from the sugar fly and read it out loud. "Princess Lolli has canceled her trip!" Raina exclaimed. She looked over at Berry. "The storm must have caused more damage in the kingdom than we thought if she is not going to Cake Kingdom."

"We should send messages to our friends to meet up now," Berry said. She wrote quick notes and handed the letters to the sugar fly. "Please take these to Dash, Melli, and Cocoa," she said. "Thank you!"

Berry watched the sugar fly soar out into the gray sky. A few of the ice patches on the ground were beginning to melt. But now that Princess Lolli had postponed her trip, Berry had to wonder what the rest of Sugar Valley looked like.

"It's a bitterly cold happening . . . ," Berry muttered as she flopped down in a chair. She

glanced around at all the books. "One of those books must have the answer," she said.

"Maybe," Raina said. "The trick is to know where to look." She blew her long bangs off her forehead. "What a mess, Berry."

"I'm sorry," Berry mumbled.

The fairies continued to do research as they waited for their friends to arrive. Berry tried not to think about what her seedlings were looking like now. Maybe the morning sun would warm up the ground and keep the seedlings safe. She hoped that her friends would get to Gummy Forest as soon as possible. This was an emergency!

The Right Spot

Not long after the sugar fly left Gummy Forest, Berry found herself surrounded by her good friends. Melli, Cocoa, and Dash had come as soon as they had heard the news. Now all five fairies were huddled up in Raina's library.

"Hot caramel," Melli said, shaking her head.

"It looks as if there was a storm in here. Who blew through here?"

"Um, that would be me," Berry confessed. "I'm desperate to find information about a spring frost." She flew up to a high shelf. "We can clean up later."

Dash picked up a pile of books from the center table. "Maybe we can search faster if we put away the books that you looked through already."

Raina gave Dash a sweet smile of thanks. "We should have a system here," she said.

"We don't have time for a system," Berry snapped. "Everyone start looking!"

Cocoa looked from Berry to Raina. She shuddered when she caught the icy stare they shared. "And I thought the patches of frozen chocolate in Chocolate Woods were bad," she mumbled.

"You know how Raina likes to keep her library," Melli whispered.

Berry saw that Raina was upset, but she couldn't stop her search now.

"This is not typical of a spring storm in Sugar Valley," Berry declared. "There have been storms to start the spring, but none like this." She flew to a shelf across the room for another book. "Maybe this book will help shed some light." She took *Shades of Spring* in her hands and flipped through the thick book.

"I can't believe you haven't found any information," Dash said. "There are so many books
here! None of them mentions a spring frost?"

Berry closed *Shades of Spring*. "I'm trying,"
she said. She didn't want to be grumpy, but
she had been researching all morning. "Sweet
strawberries, you'd think we would have found
some helpful bit of information already." She
glanced at the books lying in heaps around
the room.

"What about the other damaged crops?"
Dash asked. She popped a mint into her mouth.

"All those young seedlings and early buds are going to be ruined."

Berry felt all eyes staring at her. She wanted to be strong and show her friends that she was in control. But the weight of the day was pushing her down. Since the frost was still in Sugar Valley, Berry knew that meant the ground was still rock-hard sugar soil. There was no way her seedlings were going to grow or last.

"How are the other parts of the kingdom?" Raina asked, looking around at her friends. "I haven't been out of Gummy Forest today."

Cocoa spoke first. "I think the storm hit hardest to the north, so Candy Castle and Fruit Chew Meadow were covered in thick frost. Areas farther east weren't so bad."

Berry gasped. "Has anyone heard from

 250

Princess Lolli?" She had not even thought about the castle and what could have gone wrong there. "Maybe we should fly up to the castle and see what is going on there. I hope she is all right. Let's go!"

Berry led the way to the castle. She was sad to see the lollipop tree where they had been sitting yesterday covered in a white dusting of ice. The Royal Gardens looked sleepy and cold, buried under a thick coat of ice.

Raina reached out and gave Berry's arm a squeeze. "Let's go inside and see Princess Lolli," she said.

The palace fairies were all busy trying to spread heaters around the garden. There were no palace guards to announce their arrival. One of Princess Lolli's advisers, Tula, was standing near the front gate. Berry grabbed Raina's hand, and together they flew over to her.

"Tula," Berry said, slightly out of breath. "How is Princess Lolli?"

Tula pushed her jewel-coated glasses up on her nose. "Oh, it's a bitter day," she said. "The storm took the northern part of the kingdom by surprise."

"Is Princess Lolli . . . Is she okay?" Raina asked.

Tula regarded the two fairies standing in front of her. "Yes, she is fine," she said. "Her heart is just heavy from the weight of the storm." She unrolled a scroll in her hands. "Here is the growing list of the areas hit by the cold blast."

"How can we help?" Berry asked, jumping in.

"We're trying to figure out the damage first,"

Tula said, smiling at the fairies. "We will let you know."

Berry's wings drooped to the floor. "And Princess Lolli is not going to Cake Kingdom at all?"

Tula rolled her scroll up again tightly. "It doesn't look as if she will make that journey," she said. "So many Fruit Fairies have fruit chews and lollipops that are in danger of being ruined. The princess didn't feel it was right to leave the kingdom."

"Princess Lolli must be very disappointed," Berry said to Tula. "She was looking forward to that trip."

"Yes, I was, but I can't leave the Candy Fairies now," Princess Lolli said, coming up behind Berry.

"Berry, how are your jelly beans? How is the rest of Fruit Chew Meadow? The report this morning was not good."

Berry gasped. She hadn't thought that she'd get to see the fairy princess. She rushed over and gave her a hug. It seemed like the only thing she could do. Plus, she wanted to hide her face. She was embarrassed that Princess Lolli knew about her frozen jelly beans.

"Fairies, come closer. I know if we all work together, we'll be able to get through this difficult time," the princess said bravely.

Tula stepped forward. "Princess Lolli, you have an emergency meeting with Tangerine and JuJu. They are quite upset about the damage to their lollipops. You have to leave immediately."

"Yes, yes," Princess Lolli said, rushing off.

"Oh, I hope this blows over quickly," Tula said as they all watched Princess Lolli fly off. Tula then tucked her scroll in the satchel on her shoulder. She turned to Berry. "It's too bad," she said, full of sorrow. "Princess Sprinkle knows a lot about these storms. There have been many like this in her kingdom. I was hoping she could help. But communication has been difficult since the storm, and she is too far away to do anything for Candy Kingdom now."

Berry's ears perked up. What was Tula saying? Was there a story in the Fairy Code Book that she and her friends had missed?

"Raina," Berry whispered to her friend, "we were only looking at the history of Candy Kingdom. But what about Cake Kingdom?" Her eyes sparkled with the hope of finding a solution.

"Maybe we weren't looking in the right place!"

She raced over to her friends. They had to get back to Raina's and do more reading. Perhaps the answer was not in Candy Kingdom's history, but in a different kingdom's history.

CHAPTER 5

Sprinkle of Hope

As the five fairies made their way back to Gummy Forest, Berry flew up next to Raina.

"There must be a book that has stories just about Cake Kingdom, right?" Berry asked.

"Yes, of course," Raina said. "And I know just the book." When she got home, she went right to her library and then let out a heavy sigh. "Well,

258

I *used* to know exactly where to find the book."

Berry felt bad for Raina. Usually, Raina was able to think of a title and know exactly where the book was located. But not in this mess.

"Can I help you?" Berry asked.

"I think that you helped enough," Raina mumbled. "The book is called *Cake Kingdom: A Recipe for the Ages*," she called out. "If anyone sees it, give a holler."

Dash ducked underneath the table and brought up a strawberry-and-vanilla-colored book. "Found it!" she cried.

"What a pretty book," Melli said.

"Pretty delicious," Dash added.

Raina put the large volume on the table, and the fairy friends gathered around.

"Why didn't I think of this before?" Raina asked. She lifted the heavy cover of the book and gently turned the thin, creamy pages. "Cake Kingdom is way up north, and sure as sugar they have had spring storms like this. There are four Cake Kingdom books that go together. One of them might have the answer." Raina flipped open to the contents page. "This one doesn't talk about storms. We need the other books. . . ." Her voice trailed off. "If we can find them."

"Cocoa and I will look for the matching books," Melli offered.

"Me too!" Dash called.

Berry watched her friends scatter and search for the missing books. "I am sorry that I made such a mess," she said to Raina. She looked down at her sparkly shoes. "I am messing up everything."

"You aren't messing up *everything*," Raina told her. She smiled at her friend. "Just my library!"

"Princess Sprinkle is so wise," Cocoa said as she looked for the pink-and-white books. "I loved hearing her talk about chocolate brownies last time she was here. I hope there is an entry about one of their storms and what the Cake Fairies did to help save their sweets."

Dash rubbed her stomach. "Just thinking about Cake Kingdom is making me hungry," she said. She licked her lips. "Remember those cupcakes that Princess Sprinkle brought last time?"

"Oh, I do," Cocoa said. "Those were *choc-o-rific*!"

"And they were so beautiful," Melli added. "Remember all those clever candy toppings? She was so sweet to share with all the Candy Fairies."

"Come on," Berry pleaded. "We need to focus." She leaned closer to a book. Seeing Princess Lolli so sad had spun Berry into more of a frenzy. Now more than ever she wanted to feel as if she were helping out.

The fairies looked through and read the many history books on Cake Kingdom. Sadly, none had stories of such an early frost with any clever and warm solutions.

"I'm getting cold reading about all these frosts," Melli said. "I say we break for a snack."

"I second that!" Dash shouted. She pulled out a sack of mint treats from her bag. As she did a copy of the *Daily Scoop* fell out.

"I haven't read this week's newspaper," Cocoa said, reaching for the copy. "I heard the Sugar Pops have a new song coming out."

Berry rolled her eyes and continued reading through the thick book in front of her. She couldn't be bothered with the Sugar Pops right now.

"Wait a second," Raina said, moving closer to Cocoa. She pointed to a page in the newspaper. "Look! There was a storm at Cupcake Lake early this week," she read over Cocoa's shoulder.

Cocoa read out loud, "'There was a burst of cold that left an unexpected ice frosting over the crops.'" She looked around at all her friends. "'The soil was frozen, and the winds knocked down several stalks and trees.'"

Berry squeezed her hands together. "Remember, Tula was talking about a very recent storm!" She

 263

flew over to sit next to Cocoa. "Keep reading, Cocoa," she begged. "Maybe the article tells about a solution for frozen crops."

"Huh," Cocoa said, turning the page.

"What?" Berry said, leaning closer. "Why did you stop reading?"

"There is no answer written here. The article just ends." Cocoa scratched her head, puzzled.

Berry reached over and grabbed the paper. "How can that be?" she gasped.

"Maybe the problem was solved after the article was written," Melli offered.

Sometimes, Melli's sweet-as-caramel attitude bothered Berry, but right now, she didn't mind.

"Or maybe there is no solution," Berry said bitterly. She walked away from the table and over to the front window. She didn't want to see her friends' faces.

"Berry, we'll find a way to save the jelly beans," Dash said. "We always come up with a plan. We need a little more time."

"But we don't have time," Berry snapped. As soon as she said those words, she felt bad about her tone. She didn't mean to hurt Dash's feelings. She turned to her minty friend. "I'm sorry," she said. "I shouldn't be so harsh."

"I think we're all feeling the pressure," Melli stated.

"I just wish Princess Sprinkle were *here*," Raina said. "I bet she knows how to help the frozen crops."

Berry snapped her fingers. "Jumping jelly beans!" she exclaimed. "That's the answer! We need to bring Princess Sprinkle here to Candy Kingdom."

Melli raised her eyebrows. "That sounds like a *sugar-tastic* idea," she said. "But . . . how are we going to get Princess Sprinkle here?"

"In order to get her *here*," Cocoa said, "we need to get *there*."

"And *there* is very far!" Dash added.

Raina stood up. "Berry, Cocoa is right. We'd have to pass through the Forest of Lost Flavors. That is not a quick trip."

Berry understood the problem. But she was not going to let that ruin her plan. "If Princess Lolli was going to fly Butterscotch there, why can't we fly a unicorn there?"

"But we don't have a unicorn," Dash replied, breaking the silence.

 267

Melli shot Dash a look. "Don't be so minty," she scolded.

"It's a good point," Berry said, smiling at Dash. "I will take care of the ride," she said reassuringly. She winked at Raina. "You map out the trip."

"Berry . . . ," Raina began.

Berry held up her hand. "I will meet you back here at Sun Dip," she said, calling over her shoulder as she flew off. "This is going to be a sweet plan. You'll see!"

Berry raced to Fruit Chew Meadow to find her ride. For the first time since she had seen the frost on the leaves outside her window, she had a sprinkle of hope.

6

A Magic Ride

When Berry arrived at Fruit Chew Meadow, she saw that a layer of ice was still spread over the ground. The afternoon sun hadn't warmed up Sugar Valley enough to get rid of the ice. The sight made Berry sigh heavily. The longer the ice stayed around, the more her jelly beans were at risk of losing their flavor.

Berry tried not to let her sadness stop her. As she flew over the meadow she noticed that other Fruit Fairies had pushed the ice off the leaves of the fruit-chew plants. Berry shivered as she looked over the many different crops.

By the northern corner Berry spotted what she was looking for and flew fast. There was

beautiful Lyra, the white unicorn who guarded the fruit-chew plants.

Lyra was a small unicorn, and her sweet voice was said to be one of the secrets that made the fruit chews in the meadow so delicious. Not long ago, Mogu, the sour old troll, had tracked salt into the meadow. The salt from Black Licorice Swamp had been caked on the troll's shoes, and he had brought the salt dangerously close to Lyra. Salt was like poison to the unicorn, and she had gotten very sick.

Berry didn't like to think about that time. She was still angry at Mogu for pulling that salty stunt. But Berry and her friends had helped Lyra. She was sure that Lyra would help her and her friends now.

"Hi, Lyra," Berry called out. She patted the

unicorn and slipped her a sugar cube. Lyra's colorful mane blew wildly in the wind.

Berry noticed that Lyra looked concerned. Her extra-long eyelashes shaded her large eyes, but Berry could tell what she was thinking. This cold snap could damage her crop as well.

"The fruit chews are still covered in frost," Berry said, bending over to examine the plants. "They are the heartiest of the fruit candy, so they should be fine." She saw that the fruit chews were still colorful and the leaves were dry. "I can't say the same for my jelly beans." She shuffled her feet. "I planted a little early this year, and I am scared that I've ruined the entire crop."

Berry felt that she could be honest with Lyra. She was especially close to the unicorn. Maybe it was because they both tended to the fruit-chew

 272

candies, or just because they shared a love of fruity sweets. If Lyra said no, Berry and her friends would be in a sour state. Berry had to pose the question to Lyra in the right way. Now more than ever the fairies of Candy Kingdom needed Princess Sprinkle.

Lyra tilted her head and looked at Berry. Sensing that there was something on the Fruit Fairy's mind, she motioned for Berry to sit down near the fence.

Berry's eyes brimmed with tears as she followed Lyra. When she sat down on the chilly ground, Berry blurted out her request. "My friends and I want to go to Cake Kingdom and bring Princess Sprinkle back here."

Lyra nodded. She understood what Berry was about to ask. Berry felt that the unicorn

had even been expecting the question.

Berry looked down at her hands. "But we can't make the trip on our own. We need help. As you know, Cake Kingdom is far from here—past the Forest of Lost Flavors."

Lyra stretched her legs out beneath her.

Berry looked up at Lyra. "Would you take us?"

The white unicorn lifted her head up to the sky. Her pink-and-purple mane blew around her in a burst of color. In the stillness of the moment, Berry held her breath.

"I know it is a lot to ask of you," Berry said. "The trip for a unicorn your size could take two days." She closed her eyes and wished with all her heart that Lyra would agree to the task.

Lyra nudged Berry with her long nose. She was nodding.

Berry leaped up and hugged the unicorn tightly around her neck. "Oh, thank you, Lyra," she sang. "Raina and the others are mapping out the journey now. I know it's a big favor to ask, but I really think Princess Sprinkle will have the answer and will help Candy Kingdom."

Lyra looked toward Candy Castle and then back at Berry.

"No, we didn't talk to Princess Lolli about the trip," Berry told her. "We know she has so much else on her mind. We don't want to worry her." She smiled. "If we can get to Princess Sprinkle and show her what has happened to the crops, she can tell us what to do. Then we can tell Princess Lolli and help save the frozen candy."

The unicorn stood up and shook her body.

"Thank you, Lyra," Berry said again. "I am

going to tell the others. We'll see you tomorrow morning? We can leave from Red Licorice Lake." She gave the unicorn a hug good-bye.

Berry headed back to Gummy Forest to tell her friends the plan. She felt sure that Princess Sprinkle was the key ingredient to making this messy situation better.

CHAPTER

7

Flavorless

The next morning, Berry looked up at the sky to see the welcome and beautiful sight of a unicorn flying. Lyra's mane formed colorful ribbons across the blue sky.

"Lyra's here," Berry announced. She tucked a vine with a bunch of white jelly beans in her bag. She wanted to show Princess Sprinkle what had happened to the crop. "Is everyone ready?" she asked.

"As ready as I'll ever be," Melli said. She gripped Cocoa's hand. "I hope the trip isn't too scary."

"It might be," Cocoa told her. "But we'll all be together."

"And we'll be helping Princess Lolli and all the crops covered in ice," Raina added. "We *must* go!"

"Plus, it's so mint to ride on a unicorn!" Dash squealed, squinting up at the sky. "I can't wait!"

Raina picked up her basket of travel candy and maps. "I hope we can get to the Forest of Lost Flavors before the end of Sun Dip. It will be good to set up camp before dark."

Berry buttoned up her bag. "I think we'll make it in plenty of time," she said. "I hope these jelly beans will be safe. I want Princess Sprinkle to see the color . . . or missing color."

Lyra landed, and neighed to the fairies. One by one they hopped onto the unicorn's back and steadied themselves for the journey to Cake Kingdom.

"Everyone hold on!" Berry said, turning around to see the lineup of fairies. When she saw that everyone was holding the licorice reins, she leaned close to Lyra's ear. "We're ready to take off when you are," she said.

In a swift gallop and then a powerful leap, Lyra took flight. Her large pink wings flapped in a slow rhythm.

"This is a smooth ride," Dash said, smiling. "Not superfast, but enjoyable."

"A styling ride, for sure," Cocoa added.

As Lyra flew over Sugar Valley and they left the

familiar surroundings of Candy Kingdom, Berry couldn't help but feel a little nervous. None of her fairy friends had ever been to Cake Kingdom . . . or even seen the Forest of Lost Flavors. She knew all her friends were being very brave.

"Let's sing a song," Melli suggested. "You know Lyra loves to sing."

"Sweet idea, Melli," Berry said. She was happy to think of something besides the freezing jelly beans.

The five fairies began to sing as they sailed along the blue sky, away from Candy Kingdom. The sun moved across the sky as time went by. Berry tossed out a blanket for the fairies to wrap themselves up in. The winds had died down, but it was still chilly. After many songs and a few sweet snacks, Raina reached for Berry's sugarcoated binoculars. Only Berry would have such high-fashion travel gear!

"Sweet sugars!" Raina gasped. She was pointing straight ahead. "That must be the Forest of Lost Flavors!"

Berry straightened up. Ahead of them were tall white branches sticking up in the distance. She shuddered. Thinking about her jelly beans at home, she grew quiet. If they stayed white from the frost, they could be like this forest: flavorless.

"So mint!" Dash exclaimed as they flew over the forest. "It's creepy cool."

"Just like it said in all my books," Raina agreed.

Lyra dipped down a little lower to the ground so the fairies could see the forest. By now the sun was almost gone from the sky, which was a pale grape color.

"Good thing there is a full moon tonight," Melli said, pointing to the large moon above.

"And that I have some handy, dandy light-up-the-night mints!" Dash called. She cracked open a few mint candies as Lyra swooped above the forest.

"Does anyone live here?" Cocoa asked.

Raina put the binoculars back to her eyes. "The book said some trolls live here, but no one has ever seen them. Mogu was spotted here a few times. He has a soft spot for Cupcake Lake."

"Let's hope we don't see any trolls," Melli whispered.

Just beyond the forest was Cookie Crumble Beach, where the fairies had planned to spend the night. Lyra glided down to the rocky beach, and the fairies set up camp. Raina and Melli pitched the tents while Cocoa, Dash, and Berry prepared dinner.

"You must be tired from the flight," Berry said to Lyra. "Let me mix you up a warm, sweet dinner."

The fairies and Lyra finished up their meal. The long shadows from the Forest of Lost Flavors cast an eerie glow, and Melli huddled close to Cocoa. "This place is creepy," she said, looking around. She hugged her shawl around her waist. "I feel as if there are trolls around here," she said, her eyes wide.

"There might be," Raina said honestly. "But I think we're safe for the night."

Berry started to hum a lullaby she had once heard Lyra sing. Lyra joined in. Her soothing voice put everyone at ease and lulled the fairies to sleep. When Lyra stopped singing and lay

 285

her head down for the night, only Berry was awake. She kept thinking about how worried Princess Lolli had looked, and about the other Fruit Fairies. She peeked out of her tent and saw the white forest. Her heart sank as she thought of her own white candy.

Will Fruit Chew Meadow soon be like the Forest of Lost Flavors? she wondered. She couldn't bear the thought. What if Princess Sprinkle couldn't help them, and this was a big flop of a trip?

Berry slipped outside the tent. She flew up to a branch in a tall tree and looked out at Cupcake Lake in the distance. She hoped that tomorrow's visit with Princess Sprinkle would be as sweet as icing on a cake.

CHAPTER 8

A Sugar-Hearted Friend

Y ou can't sleep either?" Raina asked. She had
joined Berry on a branch in the moonlight. "Are
you thinking about tomorrow?"

"Yes," Berry said. She looked out in the distance.
The moon above glowed. "I can't wait to talk to
Princess Sprinkle. I remember when we met her

the last time she was in Candy Kingdom. She was so kind and wise."

"Just like Princess Lolli," Raina noted. "I am sure she will help us if she can."

Berry turned to face her friend. "Oh, Raina," she sighed. "What will Fruit Chew Meadow be like with no colorful jelly beans?" She gazed out into the white trees of the forest.

"It took years and years for the Forest of Lost Flavors to become this way," Raina said. She reached out and gave Berry's hand a gentle squeeze. "You should be prepared that Princess Sprinkle may not be able to help us."

"I know," Berry said softly. Her words left a bitter taste in her mouth, and she shuddered. She looked down at her bag lying on the ground with her jelly bean vine. A wave of courage came over her. "Princess Sprinkle will have the answer," she said, trying to be brave. "Sure as sugar, she'll be able to help me."

"Help you or *us*?" Raina asked, raising her eyebrows.

In the stillness of the night, Berry took in a deep breath. Instead of snapping at her friend, she took a moment to let Raina's words sink in. "I've been thinking of my jelly beans, but not of others," she said quietly.

"We all know how you feel about your jelly beans, Berry," Raina said. "But there were other crops affected by the weather. It didn't just happen to you."

"Yes, you're right," Berry admitted. "It feels as if the storm happened to just my crops, but I know that wasn't the only candy damaged by the storm." She sighed. "I guess I didn't take the time to ask other fairies about their candy." Berry looked down at her sparkling fingernails. "I guess I am just as sour as Razz."

"No," Raina said. "You brought us all here to find a way to fix the jelly bean jumble. And I am sure that whatever we learn from Princess Sprinkle we can use to help other fairies with their crops."

Berry reached out to hug her good friend. "Thank you," she said. "I promise I will help other Fruit Fairies. I don't want anyone to feel as helpless as I do now."

Raina stretched her arms up as she gave a wide yawn. "We should try to get some sleep. Tomorrow is a big day."

Berry drew her breath in sharply. "Don't

move!" she said. She pointed down below to her bag at the bottom of the tree. Two small trolls were sniffing around her bag–her bag with the jelly bean vine!

"Sweet sugar," Raina said with a gasp. She hugged her legs to her chest. "Do you think they saw us?"

"They definitely spotted the jelly beans," Berry said. Her heart was pounding. She had to get those trolls away from her bag!

Quietly, Berry slipped down to the end of the branch. She stuck her hand in her pocket and threw some fruit chews down, away from her bag. As Berry expected, the brightly colored candies amazed the forest trolls. She flew off the branch, sprinkling more candies down on the ground, and the trolls followed the trail away from the tree. Raina flew down and grabbed Berry's bag.

A few minutes later Berry flew back to the tree with a large grin on her face. "I still had some lemon sours in my pocket from a visit with Lemona the Sour Orchard Fairy," she said. "You should have seen those trolls pucker up when they ate one of those!"

"Serves them right for snooping around here," Raina said. She handed Berry her bag. "Maybe you should keep this in your tent tonight."

"Sure as sugar!" Berry told her. "I don't want anything to happen to these. Good night, Raina," she said, flying down to her tent.

"Sweet dreams," Raina replied before they both slipped inside warm shelter for some sleep.

"And thank you, Raina," Berry called to her.

 294

"Not just for tonight, but for everything." She flew over to give her friend a tight squeeze. "And I am sorry that I made a mess of all your books. I promise to clean that all up when we get back."

"I'll hold you to that," Raina said with a grin.

Berry felt lucky to have such a solid, sugar-hearted friend like Raina. It can be hard to point out the truth to a friend, and she was thankful that Raina had done that for her.

The next morning Berry was the first fairy up, the calls of the batter birds the first sounds she heard. Soon their loud cooing woke up all the fairies. Usually, Berry did not enjoy sleeping out. She loved all the comforts of home—including her large wardrobe and all her sparkly accessories. But she had to admit that the early morning sunrise above Cupcake Lake was stunning. The colors were so bright and created a beautiful pattern in the sky.

As she packed up her tent she thought about the trolls last night. While the fairies ate breakfast, Melli, Cocoa, and Dash heard all about the troublesome trolls.

"You tricked them," Dash said proudly.

"Well done," Cocoa told her.

Berry patted her bag. "The jelly beans are safe," she said. "Now let's see what Princess Sprinkle says about them."

Lyra sang out for the fairies to gather around her. Once again they climbed on her back, and Lyra continued the flight toward Frosted Castle. The rising sun glistened on Cupcake Lake and Frosted Castle, which jutted out from behind a wide hill. Berry noticed that the land below them looked different from Candy Kingdom. There were not as many colors dotting the landscape, and there were more hills. The castle itself was bigger than Candy Castle. It looked older and had many more rooms and towers.

"Holy peppermint!" Dash exclaimed. Her blue eyes were wide as she took in the sight below. "This is an amazing place." She rubbed her stomach. "I am getting hungry just looking around."

"I was wondering when you were going to say that," Cocoa joked. "All that frosting does look quite *choc-o-licious*!"

"With extra sprinkles," Melli added. "Just look at all those colors on the castle. This place is amazing."

"First stop, Frosted Castle," Berry said.

Lyra flew into the castle courtyard. The tall silver gates were covered with a glittering powdered sugar on top of a thick pink frosting. The five fairies climbed off the unicorn's back and looked up at the castle gates and the tall towers.

"Sweet sugar," Melli whispered.

"This place is much bigger than Candy Castle," Cocoa said, taking in the sight.

"It's much older, too," Raina stated. "This area is the oldest part of Sugar Valley."

Berry reached for the handle on the gate. "Come on," she said.

Behind the gate was a tall fairy. "Welcome to Frosted Castle," he said. He wore a round cap that looked like a cupcake and had a large welcoming smile on his face.

"I am Berry, and these are my friends," Berry said boldly. "We have traveled from Candy Kingdom, and we've come to see Princess Sprinkle."

"Welcome to Cake Kingdom," the guard replied. "I believe the princess is in the throne room." He blew a long, thin whistle, and another guard appeared. "Please take these Candy Fairies to the throne room. They are here to see Princess Sprinkle."

"Are you nervous?" Melli whispered to Berry. "I am!"

"I was more nervous about the trolls," Berry said. She reached up to fix the sugarcoated clips in her hair. "I am just hoping that Princess Sprinkle will be as sweet as her sister."

The guard flew ahead and pushed open a

door at the end of a wide hallway. "There are five Candy Fairies here to see you, Princess Sprinkle," the guard announced. He opened the door a little more and then turned back to the fairies. "She will see you now," he said.

Berry led her friends into the room. She took a deep breath. She wasn't sure what to expect from the fairy princess of Cake Kingdom.

CHAPTER
9

The Hot Spot

Princess Sprinkle was sitting on a large throne. Unlike Princess Lolli's throne, it was built up in layers and looked like a cake, with steps to reach the cushioned seat. Berry thought it looked like the drawings of wedding cakes she had seen in some of Raina's picture books. Along the top of the chair were rows of fancy sugar flowers that

Berry couldn't take her eyes off of. . . . How did those Cake Fairies get the frosted flowers so colorful and perfect?

"Hello," greeted Princess Sprinkle. Her face was similar to Princess Lolli's. The sisters looked alike except that Princess Sprinkle had long, straight brown hair instead of wavy strawberry-blond hair like her sister.

The Candy Fairies bowed their heads and said hello. Berry once again took the first step forward. "We are here because there has been a terrible storm in Sugar Valley," she told the princess.

Princess Sprinkle nodded. "Yes, I heard," she said sadly. "The news has been reported. Of course my sister was unable to make the trip to visit." She looked at each of the fairies. "How is my sister? Is everything all right? With the storm, it has been difficult to get messages to her."

Berry assured the princess that her sister was fine. "We have come to see you because we heard you recently had a storm and recovered many of your crops." She reached into her bag and pulled out her jelly bean vine. "Here is what the jelly bean crop looks like now," she said.

"Oh my," Princess Sprinkle said. She took the vine and inspected the candy. "This looks familiar. Our spring storm was not kind to our Brownie Bramble either. We had all the fairies in our kingdom working to help."

"We read about it in the *Daily Scoop*," Raina added. "I guess the story is too recent for the Fairy Code Book."

Princess Sprinkle smiled. "This was a very

recent occurrence," she said. "The storm was just a few days ago. We tried something new this time, and we seem to have saved the crops." She stepped down from her throne and motioned for the fairies to move closer to her. "You see Brownie Bramble?" She pointed out a big window to a large area to the north of the castle. "The fields were covered in ice, which freezes out the flavor," she explained.

"Bittersweet," Cocoa mumbled.

"Exactly," Princess Sprinkle said. "We had to act quickly to warm up the brownies. We placed foil on top of the crops to keep the heat in and warm the soil."

"And this foiling worked?" Berry asked, full of hope.

"Deliciously," Princess Sprinkle said. She eyed

the fairies. "Wait, does Lolli know you are here?"

Berry looked down at the ground. "Um, well, we didn't get a chance to . . ." She was searching for the right words.

"We wanted to surprise her," Raina jumped in. She looked over at Berry and winked. "We thought since she couldn't come to you, perhaps we could bring you to her and offer some help."

Princess Sprinkle grinned. "That is super-sweet of you all," she gushed. "I would love to see my sister. I was planning to send some Cake Fairies to help out with the frozen candies. The foil wrapping worked for us. I am sure it will work for the candy crops. I'd be happy to go back with you."

Berry clapped her hands. "I knew you'd be able to help us!" she cheered.

"First, we have work to do," Princess Sprinkle told them. "We had great success when we steamed up the soil. We filled large vats at Hot Cocoa Springs. The steam from the hot cocoa will keep the inside of the foil tent warm and will hopefully warm up all the candy plants in need of help."

Berry's spirits were lifting. She couldn't help herself and rushed over to Princess Sprinkle to give her a hug. The princess gave her a loving squeeze back. "What sweet fairies you are to come all this way and to care so much about your jelly beans."

Berry looked over at Raina. "This is not just about the jelly beans," she said. "This is for many of the fruit-chew crops."

"Let's take one crop at a time," the princess said wisely. "Jelly beans and other fruit candy are much more delicate than brownies and cookies."

Berry knew the weather played a big part in fruit candy flavoring. She hoped the foil would be the right cure.

Princess Sprinkle took the Candy Fairies to Hot Cocoa Springs. Berry had heard of the hot spot before in magazines and had always wanted to check it out. The springs were a popular destination for fairies to relax and soak in the warmth of the steaming hot cocoa.

"Now, this is *choc-o-rific!*" Cocoa exclaimed as they landed.

The smell of melted chocolate was heavy in the air. There were steaming springs in the ground, all bubbling with hot cocoa.

"What a sweet sight," Berry said. She saw

some fancy fairies sitting by the springs, lounging on chairs. They were all wearing very stylish clothes. Berry's mouth hung open. This was a supersweet spot. She had to admit that some of the stress of the day was melting away.

"This is a real treasure in Cake Kingdom," Princess Sprinkle said. "Many fairies come from far and wide to rest here. The springs are one of the most popular attractions here in Cake Kingdom." She looked around. "But the springs are also healing to the crops. Come, let's hurry and fill the barrels with cocoa."

"I wish we could stay here longer," Cocoa whispered to Melli. "I'd love to soak up all this chocolate."

"Maybe we'll come back one day," Melli said, watching Berry's face.

Berry smiled. "Sure as sugar, I want to come back." She glanced over at the large barrels the palace guards were rolling toward the springs. "How will we get these barrels of hot cocoa back to Candy Kingdom?"

Princess Sprinkle blew a whistle and summoned four royal Cake Kingdom unicorns. "This is Red Velvet, Marble, Pound, and Vanilla," she said. The unicorns formed a semicircle and all bowed their heads.

Berry peered up at the glorious unicorns standing before her. Like Butterscotch, they were twice the size of Lyra.

"Their names match their coats," Dash whispered, checking out the unicorns.

"Cake Kingdom unicorns are known to be the

strongest and fastest," Berry stated. She couldn't take her eyes off the handsome foursome. She noticed they were saddled with harnesses for two barrels each.

"Since these unicorns are much bigger than Lyra, they will be able to carry the extra weight," Princess Sprinkle explained.

"We'll have to fly straight to Candy Castle," Raina said. "These barrels will keep the cocoa hot, but not overnight."

"That's true," Princess Sprinkle replied. "You are a smart Candy Fairy, aren't you?"

Raina blushed. "I was just thinking out loud," she said.

"She reads a lot," Dash blurted out.

"Raina is usually right about things," Berry

added, smiling at her friend. "We want to get back to Candy Kingdom quickly. All the fruit candy crops need some warmth . . . fast."

The fairies climbed onto the backs of the majestic unicorns. Even Lyra got a ride back to Candy Kingdom on one of the unicorns. The trip back went faster, with Princess Sprinkle leading the way on her golden-cake-colored unicorn. The experienced unicorns knew short-cuts, and they flew a different route home.

As they flew over the Forest of Lost Flavors, Berry took in a sharp breath. She hoped with all her heart that the plan to warm the soil would save the fruit candy crops. The white trees and barren forest made her frightened.

She looked ahead at the lineup of unicorns and the barrels of steaming cocoa. She knew their arrival wouldn't be much of a secret. The sugar flies were going to love this bit of sweet news to spread.

"I hope this works," Berry said to her friends as they flew closer to Fruit Chew Meadow. *It has to work*, she thought.

CHAPTER 10

Sweet Endings

When they arrived at Fruit Chew Meadow, the jelly bean plants were still droopy, and all the beans were frozen. Berry knew that the jelly beans were in serious trouble.

"It's like the Forest of Lost Flavors," Dash said. Then her hand flew to her mouth. She didn't mean to sound so bitter.

Berry's eyes filled with tears. She looked to Princess Sprinkle.

"Let's get to work," the princess said bravely.

The fairies gently unrolled the sheets of foil that Princess Sprinkle had packed. They covered the freezing plants and then slipped the barrels of steaming hot cocoa underneath. When they were done with their work, the fields looked shiny in layers of foil.

"I guess we can't drink the cocoa, huh?" Dash asked. Before her friends could answer, she held up her hand. "I know what you are going to say," she laughed. "I'll chew on my mint stick."

Just as they completed the foiling, Princess Lolli appeared. She hugged her sister tightly. "When did you get here?" she asked, grinning. She squeezed her sister's hand. "I'm so happy to see you!"

"You must thank the brave Candy Fairies for my arrival here in Candy Kingdom," Princess Sprinkle told her. "They flew to Cake Kingdom and brought me back here."

Princess Lolli turned to the five Candy Fairies. "You flew all the way to Cake Kingdom?"

"Lyra took us," Berry said. "We read about Princess Sprinkle's experience with frost and knew she could help us. I wanted to show her the white jelly beans." She fluttered her wings. "I felt so bad about planting so early . . . and about the other Fruit Chew Meadow crops," she added.

Princess Lolli took Berry's hand. "You couldn't have known about the frost coming," she said. "You and your friends were very clever to go to Cake Kingdom." She smiled at her sister. "I often don't ask for help when I could use it the most. And you have proved how necessary asking for help can be."

"I'm not sure our hot cocoa plan will work," Berry said. "The jelly beans and the soil are so frozen. . . ." Her voice trailed off. "The jelly beans might be tasteless," she whispered.

"Let's not worry about that now," Princess Lolli said. "We need to wait and see how the soil responds."

The two sisters flew back to the castle to check on the other frozen crops while the fairies set out to cover the other fruit candy crops hit by the storm.

All of a sudden Razz swooped down to Fruit Chew Meadow. "What's going on here?" she asked. She stood with her hands on her hips, a disapproving expression on her face.

Berry stood up and walked over to her. This time she was going to speak her mind. "You'll see," she told her. "We have everything under control."

"Good luck," Razz spat. "Foil over freezing crops?" She threw her head back and laughed.

"Are you sure she isn't a Sour Candy Fairy?" Cocoa whispered to Berry.

At this point, Berry wasn't sure if the jelly beans would get their color and flavor back. . . . All she had now was hope. And she wasn't about to let Razz ruin that feeling.

"We are trying to save the crops," Berry said. "If you want to help spread the foil over the fruit chews and Lollipop Landing, we'd welcome your help."

Razz's mouth fell open. For the first time

Berry saw that the bitter fairy was speechless. She fluttered her wings and quickly took off.

"Wow, Berry," Cocoa said. "You really told her!"

"I was just telling the plain truth," Berry said. "Fairies who don't want to help won't be part of the celebration tomorrow."

"What celebration?" Melli asked.

Berry flew up to the sky and looped around in a graceful circle. "Yes, tomorrow the fruit-chew crops will be saved, and we will have a candy harvesting celebration."

"We can use our basket!" Cocoa exclaimed. She smiled at Melli. "We worked so hard making it, and now we can fill it with yummy jelly beans."

The next morning, when the foil was lifted from the ground, Berry kept her eyes shut tight. She didn't want to look. When she didn't hear any sounds from her friends, she opened one eye. For sure, if the jelly beans were perfect, she would have heard squealing.

"Lickin' lollipops!" she cried. All the jelly beans were white!

"Wait," Raina advised. "I think that before you panic, you should taste one. Remember that sometimes things aren't what they seem like on the outside."

Berry moved slowly over to a jelly bean vine. She carefully plucked a tiny white bean and popped it into her mouth. A burst of orange filled her mouth. "I taste orange!" she cried out. She reached farther down the row and plucked another. This time she tasted a wonderful juicy grape flavor. "Sweet sugars," she said. "The taste is there . . . but not the color."

"Winter white jelly beans." Raina grinned. "I like them!" She tossed a few into her mouth and smiled. "Well done, Berry."

The two fairy princesses arrived at the meadow. "We all need help sometimes," Princess Sprinkle said. "And I am glad that I was here to lend a hand."

"And a few barrels of cocoa," Dash added.

The two princesses laughed.

The Candy Fairies drew closer together. Seeing the sisters hug made them feel closer to one another. They had done a sweet thing. Now they could rejoice in the sweet ending to the jelly bean jumble.

Candy Fairies

Chocolate Dreams | Rainbow Swirl | Caramel Moon | Cool Mint | Magic Hearts

Gooey Goblins | The Sugar Ball | A Valentine's Surprise | Bubble Gum Rescue | Double Dip | Jelly Bean Jumble

The Chocolate Rose | A Royal Wedding | Marshmallow Mystery | Frozen Treats | The Sugar Cup | Sweet Secrets

Taffy Trouble | The Coconut Clue | Rock Candy Treasure | A Minty Mess | The Peppermint Princess | Mini Sweets

Visit candyfairies.com for games, recipes, and more!

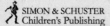